John Henry Rauch, Chigaco Academy of Science

Public Parks

their effects upon the moral, physical and sanitary condition of the

inhabitants of large cities - with special reference to the city of Chicago

John Henry Rauch, Chigaco Academy of Science

Public Parks
*their effects upon the moral, physical and sanitary condition of the inhabitants of
large cities - with special reference to the city of Chicago*

ISBN/EAN: 9783337815349

Printed in Europe, USA, Canada, Australia, Japan

Cover: Foto ©Andreas Hilbeck / pixelio.de

More available books at **www.hansebooks.com**

PUBLIC PARKS:

THEIR EFFECTS UPON THE MORAL, PHYSICAL AND
SANITARY CONDITION OF THE INHABITANTS
OF LARGE CITIES;

WITH SPECIAL REFERENCE TO THE

CITY OF CHICAGO.

By JOHN H. RAUCH, M. D.

MEMBER OF THE BOARD OF HEALTH, SANITARY SUPERINTENDENT, AND
REGISTRAR OF VITAL STATISTICS, OF CHICAGO.

1869:
S. C. GRIGGS & COMPANY,
CHICAGO.

At a meeting of the CHICAGO ACADEMY OF SCIENCES, held November 10th, 1868, the following resolution was passed:

" RESOLVED, that DR. JOHN H. RAUCH be requested, at his " earliest convenience, to prepare a paper on Public Parks, to be " read before the Academy."

Public Parks.

In compliance with the resolution of the Academy, I propose this evening to call your attention to the question of Public Parks, and their influence upon the moral, physical, and sanitary condition of the inhabitants of great cities. The benefits resulting from such dedications to public uses, have been known and appreciated by all civilized nations. And in this connection I trust that it will not be deemed out of place, if I give a brief sketch of what has been done in other cities, both ancient and modern, both at home and abroad, with a view of adornment, and of affording to the inhabitants, not only agreeable places of resort, but proving efficient aids in promoting public health.

At no period in the history of this city has this question excited so much attention as at the present time ; and it is with feelings of the deepest responsibility that I enter upon the consideration of the subject, not alone as a member of this Academy, but as the representative of the Board of Health, and as a private citizen, deeply interested in the future growth and welfare of Chicago. In treating of this subject, I lay no special claim to originality, but I shall simply state facts, allowing you to draw your own conclusions ; while, at the same time, I shall apply well-established laws and principles, which are necessary to the proper elucidation of this question in connection with the climate, topography, and diseases of this city.

The necessity for creating public parks, and on a scale commensurate with the prospective greatness of the city, is recognized by all classes of our citizens, and it is to be hoped that the action of those who are charged with the responsibility of selecting the locations, devising the plans, and providing the means for securing these results, may prove wise and judicious, and thus receive the commendations of posterity.

"Best is Pelasgicum empty,"

was wisely expressed by the Pythian oracle, thereby denoting that every large and populous city, as well as Athens, should have its

Pelasgicum, or vacant pieces of ground, serving as so many reservoirs of pure air, for counteracting the contaminating atmospheric influences incident to cities, and the effect of epidemics and contagions. In order more thoroughly to appreciate the full import of these words, it may be proper to refer to the circumstances from which they derive their origin. According to Pausanius, Pelasgicum was the name given to the most ancient part of the fortifications of the Acropolis at Athens, from having been constructed by the Pelasgii, (or "wall builders," as they were called,) who, in the course of their migrations, settled in Attica, and were employed by the Athenians in the erection of these walls. The rampart raised by this people, often mentioned in the history of Athens, included a portion of the ground below the wall, at the foot of the rock of Acropolis. This had been allotted to the Pelasgii while they resided at Athens, and owing to the conspiracy formed by them against the Athenians, they were banished; and such was the abhorrence with which this conspiracy was regarded, that an execration was pronounced on any who should build houses on this ground. In consequence of this execration, it was not built upon; and thus being necessarily left vacant, the beneficial effects of this open space in the course of time became so apparent that the Pythian oracle uttered,

" Best is Pelasgicum empty ;"

and what was supposed, at the time, to have been a great curse, proved ultimately to be a blessing in disguise.

May not such be the case with regard to our own city? We have already built up its surface from a morass, thus securing a well-devised system of drainage, and it is believed, and I think I am not stating too much, that, by making use of our local topography, we can create parks which shall become the ornament of the city, and a blessing to its inhabitants.

Parks have been aptly termed "the lungs of a city." They are emphatically the people's gardens,—places to which the overtasked laborer and mechanic of the overcrowded city can, with his wife and children, resort to breathe the breath of God's pure air, inhale the odors of fresh, blooming flowers, and enjoy the pleasures of a rural retreat on a larger scale, amid far richer vegetable forms, than in the gardens created by mere private opulence.

That the people of this country have a keen love of nature, and of the beautiful in art, is evidenced by the general interest taken in this subject, and the success which has attended the laying out of the Central, Fairmount, Prospect, Druid Hill, and other parks in this country. This feeling is extending, and as the squares which are found in nearly all our cities no longer satisfy the longings of the inhabitants, who now demand the laying out of hundreds of acres in a style proportionate to the hopes and expectations of the future of the locality. The immense throng that daily resort to such places, — not simply the millionaire, or the aristocratic merchant, but the laborer, the mechanic, and those from the humblest walks of life, coupled with the decorousness of their behaviour, and their cheerful compliance with the necessary regulations, — all attest the popularity and beneficial influence of such dedications. Can we not have such resorts in Chicago?

It is true that we have not that relief and depression of soil, of ledgy rock and deep valley, which are to be found in the Central and other parks of this country ; but we can have ample drives, graveled walks, fountains, lakes, and all the forms of vegetable and animal life which have been acclimated in our latitude. We can have parks which shall be the ornament and pride of the city ; where, by easy access, our people can enjoy the beauties of nature, and all the pleasures of landscape gardening.

If we analyze the sources of our happiness, we shall find that they are reducible to two—external and internal ; but while it is from the external world that we derive all our ideas, the office of reflection and of imagination is performed in the interior world of thought. Man, however much he may boast of the superiority of mind over matter, is as sensitive to external changes as the barometer is to those of the atmosphere. A pleasing landscape or a bright sunshine exhilerates his spirits, while a dreary waste, or a leaden sky produces depression. We associate these ideas of external nature with our present sources of happiness or misery, and carry them into our conceptions of a future state.

Hence, in every age, and among every nation, whether Christian or Pagan, who have made any progress in intellectual development, the idea of Paradise has been one not purely of mental culture, of converse and friendship, but one in which the sensuous nature was largely to participate.

Milton has described the abode of our first parents as a combination of sensuous delights, with a gorgeousness of word-painting

which has never been surpassed.—trees of noblest kind, amid which
stood the " Tree of Life,"

> " High, eminent, blooming ambrosial fruits of vegetable gold;"

fresh fountains, watering with many a rill, flowers worthy of
Paradise, and

> " Rolling on Orient pearl;"

groves whose trees wept odorous gums and balms; lawns, and
palmy hillocks, and flocks grazing the herb; and

> " Flowers of all hue, and without thorn the rose;"

umbrageous grottos, and caves of cool recess, o'erarched with
mantling vine; murmuring waters falling down the hill-slope, with
banks myrtle-crowned; birds making vocal the woods; and vernal
air breathing the smell of field and grove. Such was deemed the fit
residence of our great progenitors before the Fall.

The Elysium of the ancients was a union of leafy bowers, flowery
meads, and murmuring brooks, fanned by a genial air, and lighted
by another sun and other stars.

Mahomet, while creating a voluptuous paradise, has brought in
as accessories, groves, fountains, and rivers of bliss; and Christian
congregations do not hesitate to join with fervor in singing that
beautiful hymn,

> " Sweet fields beyond the swelling flood,
> Stand dressed in living green."

These examples show how intimately the forms of external
nature are associated, not only with our happiness here, but hereafter; and how deeply they are impressed upon man, whether in a
savage or civilized state.

From the earliest period of history, a love of nature and landscape
gardening has been fostered and encouraged in the same ratio as
civilization has advanced. The Jews and Egyptians had their gardens; and Nebuchadnezzar, to gratify his wife Amytis, a daughter
of the king of Medea, who was home-sick, and longed for the picturesque scenery and mountains of her native land, constructed the
famous hanging gardens of Babylon. The captive Jews, Phœnicians,
Syrians, and Egyptians were engaged for years in building such
works; and, according to Diodorus and Strabo, nothing had been
attempted prior to their time to compare, in magnificence and
grandeur, with what was then accomplished. Among the ruins of
Ninevah, Layard found traces of gardens; also, a large tree, which,
from its surroundings, he inferred had been an object of adoration.

The Chinese paid considerable attention to the ornamenting of their gardens, and at one time their attempts at landscape gardening were more successful than those of any other nation. To them may be traced what is now called the natural system, so much in vogue in England, and which has been generally adopted in this country.

A deep love of nature pervaded the minds of the Hindoos, as is manifest in their public grounds and gardens. There was nothing striking in the gardens of the Persians, no doubt owing to the want of grand and natural scenery. They were regarded as places of luxurious repose, and were constructed wholly in reference to this end. Trees were planted in rows, in order that the wind might draw its currents through them ; fountains were interposed, and streams ran through them to increase the sensation of coolness. Flowers were cultivated for perfume and beauty, with here and there a terebinthinate evergreen, which was regarded by them as a great luxury. These gardens were generally surrounded by an enclosure.

" The Greeks," according to Humboldt, " regarded the vegetable world as standing in a manifold and mythical relation to heroes and to the gods, who were supposed to avenge every injury inflicted on the trees and plants sacred to them. Imagination animated vegetable forms with life, but the types of poetry, to which the peculiar direction of mental activity among the ancient Greeks limited them, gave only partial development to natural scenery."[*] Homer, Pinder, Sophocles, and Euripedes occasionally indulge in descriptions of nature.

Their ideas of landscape gardening, while derived from the Persians, were much improved upon. They encouraged art more than nature. Athens had its public park, called ACADEMIA. It was laid out by Cimon, who formed pleasant walks, introduced water and planted groves. At the entrance an altar dedicated to Love was placed, and scattered through the grounds were statues and monuments of the most worthy citizens. One portion of this park was devoted to the exercise of athletic games, and another to contemplative recreation. Greek civilization made its impress on the Romans, and in many respects they were similar, showing that their love of nature was not entirely lost sight of by their love of art. Cicero and Pliny delighted in descriptions of nature ; and in the poetic works of Virgil, Horace, and Tibullus, frequent allusions to natural scenery occur. Lucan gives an admirable description of the destruction of a Druidic forest on the now treeless shores of Marseilles. Rome,

---

[*] *" Cosmos."*

when in her glory, was proud of her rural retreats and pleasure grounds, which were laid out with walks and drives for chariot and horseback exercises, with enclosures for wild beasts, apiaries, flower-gardens, and fountains flowing from marble vases.   The park proper, in the immediate vicinity of the houses, was formal and symmetrical with the architecture, and the walls were lined with box and plane trees, sheared to the shape of the walls.   From the description of the younger Pliny of his Tusculan villa, we are led to infer that the principal object of Roman landscape gardening was its effect upon the perspective ; as here everything was arranged with reference to the best distant views of the Campagna.   In fact the same is the case with the grounds and gardens of Italy at the present day, the artistic preponderating over the natural.

The Arabs, when at the height of power and civilization, paid some attention to landscape gardening, and carried with them their tastes into Spain.   This is shown by the fact that the Caliph Ab durrahman I. himself laid out a botanical garden at Cordova, and caused rare seeds to be collected by his own travelers in Syria and other countries of Asia.   He planted, near the palace of Rissafah, the first date-tree known in Spain, and sang its praises in a poem, expressive of plaintive longing for his native Damascus.

Prescott, in his "Conquest of Mexico," says, "There is no doubt, from the accordant testimonies of Hernan Cortes, in his reports to the Emperor Charles V., of Bernal Diaz, Gomara Ovieda, and Hernandez, that at the time of the conquest of Montezuma's Empire there were no menageries and botanic gardens in any part of Europe, which could be compared with these of Huaztepec, Chepultepec, Iztapalapan, and Tezuco."   Humboldt saw two trees (*Taxodium disticha*—Linn.) near Chepultepec, which he supposed to be the remnants of an ancient garden or pleasure-ground of Montezuma's, which measured thirty-eight feet in circumference.

In France, Germany, and England, landscape gardening received but little attention for many years, and their imitations of the Roman and Italian styles were poor, leaving but little of the artistic.   The Dutch school at one time was foremost.   It was a revival of the ancient or geometric style, in which statues, vases, and busts were interspersed with fountains, and the various forms of the vegetable kingdom.

Landscape gardening is a word of modern coinage, first used by the poet Shenstone.   In England but little attention was paid to the art of gardening until the time of Addison, when Bridgeman, the court gardener, in the palace grounds at Kensington, acted upon the suggestions received from the descriptions of travelers of the imitations of nature which the Chinese made use of in their gardens. Pope, in his garden at Twickenham, laid aside formality, imitating the natural. Addison's garden at Rugby was informal without being picturesque. "Kent was the first man who really formed a landscape, sweeping away the rubbish which represented the ancient style. He undertook the creation of scenery upon the ground at his command, on the same principles that he would select a subject in nature for his canvas. The radical change which followed witnessed the destruction of noble avenues and terraces by the imitators of Kent, in order to demonstrate the capabilities of the ground, and landscape gardening soon became a mechanical business instead of an art, which Kent had made it." *

It was not until after the publication, by Gilpin, of his various "Picturesque Views," and the "Essays on the Picturesque," by Sir Uvedale Price, in which the true principle of art applicable to the creation of scenery, was laboriously studied and carefully defined, that a revival of the art took place. The poetry of Shenstone, Mason, and Knight assisted in bringing about this result. The most distinguished English landscape gardeners that have flourished since the commencement of the last century, have been Humphrey Repton, who died in 1818, and John Claudius Loudon, who died in 1843. They developed and carried to its greatest perfection the modern or natural style of landscape gardening, as is evidenced at Blenheim, the seat of the Duke of Marlborough ; Chatsworth, the seat of the Duke of Devonshire, where there are scenes illustrative of almost every style of the art; and also at Woburn Abbey; Ashbridge ; and Arundel Castle. More recently the writings of Paxton and Kemp have done much to improve and foster this taste among the English. Soon after the adoption of the natural style in England, it became fashionable upon the Continent; "yet, in the neighborhood of many of the capitals, especially those of the south of Europe, the taste for the geometric or ancient style prevails to a considerable extent; partially, no doubt, because that style admits, with more facility, of those classical and architectural accompaniments of vases, statues, busts, etc., the passion for which pervades a people rich in ancient and modern sculptural works of art. Indeed, many of the gardens on the Continent are more striking

---

* Downing: "*Landscape Gardening.*"

from their numerous sculpturesque ornaments, interspersed with fountains and *jets d' eau*, than for the beauty or rarity of their vegetation, or from their arrangement." *

The name PARK is derived from the French *parque, parc,* (*i. e.,* a *locus inclusus,*) formerly a large quantity of ground inclosed and privileged for the keeping of beasts of the chase, particularly the deer. by the King's grant or prescription. These grants were made by the kings of England to the nobles; and as the country became populated, these parks were selected as residences, and in the course of time were considered as luxurious appendages to the dwellings of the rich.

The word park has different significations, but that in which we are now interested has grown out of its application, centuries ago, simply to hunting grounds; the choicest lands for such purposes being those in which the beasts of the chase thrived best, and consequently were most abundant. Sites were chosen, in which it was easy for them to turn from rich herbage to clear water, from warm sunlight to cool shade; that is to say, by preference, ranges of well-watered dale-land, broken by open groves, and dotted with spreading trees, undulating in surface, but not rugged. In some parts of Britain the word park is still employed in its original sense— to denote a field or enclosure; but more generally applied to the enclosed grounds around a mansion, designated in Scotland by another term of French origin—*policy*. The park, in this sense, not only includes the lawn, but all that is devoted to the growth of timber, pasturage for deer, sheep, etc., in connection with the mansion, and to pleasure walks or drives, or to purposes of enjoyment, in contradistinction to those of economical use. Gay parties of pleasure occasionally met in these parks, and when these meetings occurred, the enjoyment otherwise obtained in them was found to be increased. Hence, instead of mere hunting-lodges and hovels for game-keepers, extensive buildings and accommodations, devoted frequently to festive purposes, were, after a time, provided within the enclosures. Then it was found that people took pleasure in them without regard to the attractions of the chase, or of conversation; and this pleasure was perceived to be, in some degree, related to the scenery, and in some degree to the peculiar manner of appreciation which occurred in them; and this was also found to be independent of intellectual gifts, tranquilizing and restorative to the powers most tasked in ordinary social duties, and stimulating only in a healthy

* Downing : " *Landscape Gardening.*"

and recreative way to the imagination. Hence, after a time, parks began to be regarded, and to be maintained with reference, more than to anything else, to the convenient accommodations of numbers of people, desirous of moving for recreation among scenes that should be gratifying to the taste or imagination. Hagley Park, for many years, was considered the finest in England, although there are many there now much handsomer, averaging from one to five miles in diameter; and many of them are open to the public with slight restrictions. As the power of the people has increased the Royal Parks have been more adapted to their wants.

In the present century, not only have the old parks been thus maintained and improved, but many new parks have been formed exclusively for the purposes of recreation, enjoyment, and health, especially within and adjoining considerable towns; and it is upon our knowledge of the latter that our simplest conception of a town park is founded.*

Nearly all the towns, villages, and cities have their pleasure-grounds in some form, or private parks open to them. In addition, all have their cricket-grounds and commons, where the old meet to gossip, and the young to indulge in various athletic games.

___

PARKS OF GREAT BRITAIN.

The public parks of London are Kensington Garden, 262 acres; Hyde Park, 389 acres; Green Park, 55 acres; St. James Park, 59 acres (all of which are connected in a chain, though partly separated); Regent's Park and Primrose Hill, 473 acres; Battersea Park, 175 acres; and Kensington Park containg 55 acres.

The Royal Parks in the vicinity of London are also much resorted to:—Windsor, 3,800 acres; Hampton Court and Burley, 1,812 acres; Richmond, 2,468 acres; and the Royal Gardens at Kew, 684 acres. Epping Forest and others are easily reached, making 3,000 acres in the city, and about 11,000 in the vicinity that are open to the public.

The grounds of the Horticultural Society and the Crystal Palace are open to the public for a small entrance fee. Victoria Park is among the most frequented; here 130,000 visitors have been counted in one day. The fashionable drive of London is the Ring-Road, in Hyde Park, three miles long and from twenty-seven to sixty feet wide; and another of a mile long and thirty-six feet wide. The fashionable riding avenue is in this park, and is ninety feet wide and

___

*Olmsted.

a mile in length.   There is not much room for riding or driving in the other parks.

Phœnix Park, in Dublin, contains 1,752 acres, and is one of the best natural parks in the world, but is not well laid out or well kept.   Birkenhead Park, near Liverpool contains 182 acres, designed and constructed by Sir Joseph Paxton and Mr. Kemp, and is one of the best laid out and most complete, for its age, in Europe.   Several new ones have been laid out, with villa districts about them, connected by broad pleasure drives, upon which, in 1867, $1,640,000 were expended.

Birmingham has a park recently laid out, where an entrance fee of a penny is charged, by which funds are raised to defray the expenses incident to its purchase and maintenance.   As soon as paid for, admission will be free.   Halifax has fine parks, Derby and Arboretum, both of which were provided by benevolent citizens. Manchester, Bradford, and other manufacturing towns have recently laid out parks, the result of subscriptions or joint-stock companies Public promenades are common in England, among which may be cited the old city walls and the river bank above the town of Chester, the common and old castle grounds at Ludlow, the castle garden and cathedral grounds at Hereford, the river banks at Lincoln, and the cathedral green at Salisbury and Winchester.

PARKS ON THE CONTINENT.

The garden of the Tuileries, with the Champs Elysees, in Paris, makes the finest urban promenade in the world.   In the centre is an avenue of horse chestnuts three miles in length.   On either side, in the gardens, are groves, shrubberies, and *parterres* of flowers.   The garden of the Luxembourg is another interior promenade laid out in formal style, with an avenue, groves, flower beds, and a rose garden of a mile in circumference.   The gardens of the Louvre are also very fine.   There are also many other gardens and squares in Paris. Many of the streets are planted with trees.   Some of the *boulevards* are the levelled ramparts planted with trees.   The *boulevards exterieurs* are an interrupted series of broad streets, of an aggregate length of seventeen miles, lined with trees.

The avenue de L' Imperatrice is a straight promenade between Paris and the Bois de Boulogne, three hundred feet wide.   It consists of a carriage way sixty feet wide, a pad for saddle horses, and a graveled walk on either side, each forty feet wide ; on the outside of all is a slope of turf, planted in the rear with a group of trees and shrubs in the natural style ; back of this, on both sides, is a narrow road adapted to traffic, which also gives access to a line of detached villas.

The famous Bois de Boulogne is an ancient royal forest in the suburbs of Paris. It remained nearly in its natural state until 1855, when Napoleon III. commenced its improvement, and this work is now regarded as one of his most popular acts. It contains 2,158 acres, thus divided : wood, 607 acres ; open turf, 875 acres ; water, 174 acres ; roads, 365 acres ; nurseries and flower-beds, 171 acres ; length of carriage road, 36 miles ; bridle path, 7 miles ; and walks, 16 miles. The Bois de Vincennes is a natural forest, the improvement of which was commenced several years ago, but discontinued, and is now chiefly used for reviewing troops and for artillery purposes. Work has recently been commenced on it again. Menceau and Buttes de Chaumont are new parks, which are very popular—the last being quite unique in design. The Jardin des Plants, a zoological as well as botanical garden, near Paris, is much frequented.

At Frankfort, Leipsic, and Vienna, pleasure grounds have been provided by razing the wall, and filling the moat, and by the skillful arrangement of the materials, making the ground-work of a garden in the natural style. In other cities the leveled ramparts have been made into broad roads, bordered with trees. The Boulevards of Brussels are straight streets, 125 feet wide, with rows of trees between them, a walk 21 feet wide ; carriage-road, 36 feet wide ; a soft graveled horseback road, 21 feet wide ; a business road, 30 feet wide, with a flagged walk for rainy weather. Houses are on these boulevards, in front of which are private gardens, or fore-courts. Brussels has also an old park, and two botanical and zoological gardens.

The Prater is the principal rural promenade at Vienna, and has a straight carriage-road over a mile in length, with a walk on one side, and an equestrian pad on the other. Near the city it contains a great number of coffee and play houses ; but being five miles in length, portions of it are thoroughly secluded and rural. At one time it was the most frequented park in the world, the Bois de Boulogne and the Central Park being more frequented at this time.

Munich has its Hofgarten, or Royal Park, and the English garden which was laid out under the direction of Count Rumford, and
is about four miles long, and a half mile wide. The Sonnenstrasse
in this city is a beautiful street—in fact one of the handsomest in
Europe.

The Thiergarten, at Berlin, contains over 200 acres, laid out in
straight drives and walks. The Prussian Royal Gardens of Sans
Souci, Charlottenberg, and Heiligensee, are extensive grounds,
though rather stiff and formal in appearance. Fine public grounds
are also to be found in Dresden, Stuttgart, Hanover, Brunswick,
Baden, Cassel, Darmstadt, Gotha, Weimar, Schwœtzingen, Toplitz,
Prague, and Hamburg. Those of Antwerp, the Hague, and War-
saw are remarkable for their beauty. In all German public gardens,
coffee-houses are an adjunct, and music is furnished by the government.

The summer gardens of St. Petersburgh are very fine, though
not large, and are kept in the most careful manner. Among these
is the Catherinehoff, a perfect gem, and the fashionable promenade
of the city. Many of the islands of the Neva contain pleasant
gardens, and the Tzenskoe Selo is one of the most remarkable in the
world. It is the residence of the Imperial family, and consists of
350 acres.

Stockholm has many pleasant walks, and the Djingard, or deer
park, is beautifully kept and three miles in circumference. The
Haga Park is picturesque, having water communication with its
different parts and with the city. Copenhagen contains many places
of public resort, but the most notable promenade is the royal deer
park, (Dyrhave,) a noble forest.

In Italy the chief public resorts are the gardens attached to
the villas. The Cascine of Florence, on the banks of the Arno,
commands fine views, and the drive on the Pincian Hill at Rome,
has magnificent views in the distance. The fashionable drive at
Naples is on a broad street called the Riviera di Chiaja, near the
bay, but separated from it by a public garden.

Nearly all the Spanish and Portuguese towns are provided with
promenades.

LANDSCAPE GARDENING IN THE UNITED STATES.

In this country, until recently, but little attention has been paid
to landscape gardening, and nearly all the improvements of the

grounds of our finest country residences have been made under the direction of the owners themselves, suggested by their own good taste, in many instances improved by the study of European authors, or by personal inspection of the finest places abroad. The first botanical garden was laid out and planted by John Bartram, one of the pioneer botanists of this country, near Philadelphia. Some of the trees planted by him are still to be seen ; among them the enormous cypress, the destruction of which he feared by the British army after the battle of Brandywine, which so much preyed upon his mind that his death was hastened by it. Humphrey Marshall also laid out a botanical garden near West Chester, Pa.

One of the most celebrated places, known as the " Woodlands," the seat of the Hamilton family, near Philadelphia, was perhaps the best specimen of landscape gardening in this country in the early part of the present century. These grounds were for a long time under the care of the distinguished botanist Pursh.

Judge Peters's seat, live miles from Philadelphia, was, fifty years ago, the finest representative of the geometric, or ancient style, in America. One of the chief attractions of this place, which still exists, is a fine avenue of hemlocks, planted 120 years ago, several with English ivy, also a chestnut tree planted by Washington, still in full vigor.

Lemon Hill, a short distance above the Fairmount Water Works, on the Schuylkill river, was, thirty years ago, the most perfect specimen of the geometric mode in this country. Through the liberality of Mr. Pratt it was open to the public.

Clermont, on the Hudson, then the residence of Chancellor Livingston, was laid out in the geometric style, with a decided French impress, and at one time was quite noted.

Waltham House, about nine miles from Boston, was, forty years ago, one of the finest places in the country. The park, in addition to clusters of native wood, was enriched with English limes and elms, watered by a fine stream, and well stocked with deer.

The first work published in this country on landscape gardening was the American Gardener's Calendar, by Bernard McMahon, of Philadelphia ; and the only practitioner of any note was M. Parmentier, of Brooklyn, who emigrated to this country in 1824. He gave to landscape gardening quite an impetus, and to his taste and skill we are indebted for many of the magnificent places on the Hudson ; also others in different States and Canada. The taste for rural improvement was slowly and gradually increasing, and the evidence of the growing wealth and prosperity of our citizens manifested itself in the increase of elegant cottages and villa residences on the banks of our noble rivers, along our rich valleys, and wherever nature seems to invite by her rich and varied charms. This feeling or taste for improvement is contagious, and once fairly appreciated and established in one portion of the country, it soon became disseminated in other portions, until it has now become quite general.*

The progress that landscape gardening has made during the last twenty-five years is truly astonishing, and to no one are we so much indebted as to the lamented Downing. The impress of his genius is visible everywhere, and monuments to his taste and skill are to be found throughout the entire land. On the Hudson are to be found some of the finest specimens of the art, and nowhere in the Union is it so far advanced.

The environs of Boston are more highly cultivated than those of any other city in North America; in fact, in certain directions the whole neighborhood may be considered a landscape garden. In the neighborhood of Baltimore are found a number of fine old places, several of them being as elaborate and magnificent as any in the country. Others are to be found scattered throughout different States, even in sections comparatively new, showing conclusively that a taste for the beautiful in art and nature is fast being disseminated among the people.

It is only a few years since the establishment of rural cemeteries was commenced in the United States, owing to the crowded and confined state of our burial grounds within the large cities and their manifest injurious influence upon health. Such has been the progress of this movement, and its importance and necessity so apparent, that it has been almost universally adopted, and intramural interments, under any circumstances, in many of the cities are totally prohibited. As a legitimate result, arising from the growing taste for landscape gardening and the promptings of affection and respect for the memory of the sacred dead, we have in the United States the finest rural cemeteries in the world, which we think may be regarded as a sure evidence of our advancement in civilization and enlightenment.

---

* Downing's "*Landscape Gardening.*"

PARKS AND PUBLIC GROUNDS IN THE UNITED STATES.

We have, however, no finished parks in the United States, and it is only within recent date that much attention has been paid to this subject. It is true that there is scarcely a town that does not have its square or promenade, but in its European signification there are but few that deserve that appellation. Although there is probably not a village, town, or embryo city laid out that does not devote a portion of it for public uses, still the importance of such resorts and their proper improvement is not thoroughly appreciated. This, no doubt, arises from various causes; among them. in certain sections, the sparseness of population and the absence of wealth and the active life led by a majority of our people, who take comparatively no time for recreation or pleasure, little dreaming of the expenditure of mental and physical force incident to such a life, and the premature decay which inevitably follows ; also, the false utilitarian views taken by many of the subject.

BOSTON AND NEW ENGLAND.

The " Common," so long the boast and delight of Boston, is a small park of forty-eight acres of ground, of an undulating character, surrounded by an iron railing, in which are found about 1,300 trees, nearly all of them having been planted. It dates to 1634, and by a clause in the city charter it is made public property forever, and cannot be sold or exchanged. There are many walks in it, laid out more with a view of communicating with entrances from all directions, than any attempt at the picuresque. The walks are spacious, shaded by magnificent trees over a century old ; the one on Beacon street being particularly unique and pleasant. The public garden, which was once a portion of the Common, is now separated from it by Charles street, and will soon rival it for beauty and usefulness.

Throughout the New England States the public grounds of many of the towns are planted with trees without much arrangement or order, showing chiefly the beauty and value which the trees acquire by age. This is particularly the case with Cambridge, New Haven, Springfield, Portland, Hartford and Northampton ; in fact, the principal charm of many of the villages is the trees that line the streets. Among the most striking may be mentioned Hadley, Deerfield and Norwich.

The many noble elms that are found in the public grounds and streets of New Haven, which were planted mainly through the instrumentality of Hillhouse, at the close of the eighteenth century, have justly obtained for that city the soubriquet of the " City of Elms." There are at New Haven several public squares. The Wooster, containing five acres, is laid out with taste ; the Green, containing sixteen acres, shaded by its graceful and elegant elms ; and the Brewster park, containing fifty-five acres.

At Providence there is a park planted with elms, nearly a mile in circumference, around a cove of the Providence river. The public park at Hartford has not been what might be termed a success, owing to its being laid out on a difficult piece of ground, with an ill-digested plan.

PHILADELPHIA.

The public squares of Philadelphia have long been the pride of that city. Independence Square, in the rear of Independence Hall, is one of the oldest and finest. Washington square, in olden times, was the Potter's Field, where, during the Revolutionary war, over two thousand soldiers of the American Army, who had died from wounds and camp-fever, were buried. It was last used as a place of interment during the prevalence of yellow fever in 1793, and was finally closed in 1795, and laid out as a public square in 1815. In this square is laid the foundation of a monument to Washington. Franklin square is kept in good order, and is mainly distinguished for the deer, squirrels and peacocks that are kept in it. Penn, Rittenhouse, Logan, Fairhill and Norris squares are of more recent origin, all being well cared for and kept in a tasteful manner. The grounds in the vicinity of the Fairmount Water Works, on the Schuylkill river, are tastefully laid out, and for years have been a favorite resort. Several years ago, Lemon Hill, about a half mile from the waterworks, was purchased and laid out as a public park. It was at one time the handsomest villa in America, containing 120 acres, to which additions have been made of 80 acres. The alterations were designed by Messrs. Sidney and Adams. These, with the magnificent trees and fine natural position, make it already a delightful place. Additions to the grounds have since been made on the opposite side of the river, which are being improved, and will soon be connected by a bridge over the Schuylkill.

An act was passed at the last session of the Legislature of Pennsylvania, increasing the boundaries of Fairmount park, on both sides of the Schuylkill, and including a portion of the ground lying on the banks of the romantic Wissahickon, making a total area of 2,700 acres. Philadelphia has lately received as a "Christmas gift" from Jesse George and his sister, Rebecca George, eighty-three acres, known as "George's Hill," on the west side of the Schuylkill. With these additions it will not be presumptuous on the part of Philadelphia to claim that no city of this continent, and probably of the world, has more natural advantages and unsurpassed beauty than are included within the limits of Fairmount park.

WASHINGTON.

Recently, considerable attention has been paid to the improvement and care of the grounds attached to our colleges, hospitals, and other public buildings. We are greatly indebted to the late Downing, for the taste and skill displayed in the arrangement of the public grounds at Washington, particularly those of the Smithsonian Institute and LaFayette Square. The grounds of the Capitol and those of the White House have long been favorite promenades.

The project of a new mansion for the President, and of the establishment of a great National Park, has been frequently agitated, while the engineer officers have already examined the topography of the country adjacent to Washington for this purpose. Mr. Corcoran has offered to donate a large tract of land upon certain conditions. It is thought that at least 1,800 acres of ground lying east of Rock Creek, and north of Columbia College, will be selected, as it is well adapted by nature for the purpose contemplated, and can be improved at comparatively small expense.

It has also been proposed to make this park a working model of the United States, "to delineate, if not reproduce in miniature, the topography of the Continent ; to set Huron and Ontario in reduced scale upon a living map some two miles long, not in water colors, but in the element itself ; to lead a toy Mississippi from its baby nursery through a little continent to a small Gulf of Mexico. The St. Lawrence and the Colorado, and all other great rivers, are to be represented by mimic streams, and all the States and Territories are to be represented, preserving their relative position and proportion. It is also proposed that museums shall be erected upon each of these little representative tracts, and the States and citizens shall be invited to contribute to their cabinets, specimens of the natural and artificial productions of the States represented."

I hope that nothing of the kind will be attempted, for it will most surely result in failure, as landscape gardening cannot be successfully restricted to such arbitrary rules. There are plenty of other ways by which its national character can be shown, and every portion of our country represented, in full consonance with the beautiful in art and nature.

NEW YORK.

The Central Park of New York is one of the largest and most important works of the kind, not alone in this country but the world. The genius of Downing laid the foundation for it, but it was not until after his death that the ground was appropriated for this purpose by an act of the Legislature of New York, and it was not until the close of 1857 that the actual purchase of the land was completed. Premiums for designs amounting to $4,000 were at this time offered by the Commissioners intrusted with the conduct of the enterprise, and early in June, 1858, the plan submitted by Fred. Law Olmsted and Calvert Vaux was adopted by the board, after extraordinary competition, thirty-five studies having been presented, and some of them from Europe.

The park is two and one-half miles long and half a mile wide, and is being formed in two parts, connected by a narrow strip of ground containing the old and new reservoirs for supplying the city with water; the former a quadrangular basin of mason work, the latter of an irregular curved outline, with an earth embankment to retain the water—in all covering about 150 acres. The original park inclosure contains 776 acres, to which have been added 68 acres at one time, and more recently Manhattan square; so that it now contains 862 acres. It is laid out in the first place, to obtain a large unbroken surface of smooth meadow-like ground, even where the natural obstacles to this mode are to be overcome by heavy expenditures. The immediate borders of these spaces are planted in a manner to hide or disguise any incongruous quality in the grounds beyond. The rocky and broken surface which originally characterized the whole site, however, admits of the application of this evident preference of the designers to but a small portion of the grounds, while elsewhere its capacities for picturesque effect have been revealed. The different classes of communication are so arranged that by a peculiar system of arched passages, it never becomes necessary for a person on foot to cross the surface of the carriage track, or the horseman to cross the carriage roads, though he may ride on them if he prefer.*

---
*Olmsted.

The following statistics show how the land is appropriated. Area occupied by carriage roads 49 acres, 9 miles in length; by bridle roads 15 acres, 5 miles in length; by walks 38 acres, 25½ miles in length; making a total of 103 acres; by rock surface, mainly without soil or shrubbery, 24 acres; by park ground fertilized or chiefly fertilized, and in trees, shrubbery, or in open lawns, exclusive of reservoirs, roads, walks, pads, rock surface, &c., 536 acres.

The subjoined statistics show that the enhanced value of property, by the laying out of such works is more than ample to meet the interest on the cost of construction :

Increased value of property in XII, XIX, and XXII Wards since 1856,................................		$75,675,750.00
The rate of tax for 1867 is 2.67, yielding in the increased valuation above stated an increased tax of		$2,020,542.53
The total expenditures for construction from May 1, 1857, to January 1, 1868, is	$5,185,299.11	
The cost of land of the Park to the City, is.....	5,028.844.10	
Total cost of Park up to this time,.............		$10,214,143.21
The annual interest on the cost of the land and improvement of the Park up to this time at six per cent.	$612,848.58	
Deduct one per cent. on $399,300 of the above stock, issued at five per cent.................	$3,993.00	
		$608,855.58
Excess of increased tax in three wards over interest in cost of land and improvements,....		$1,411,686.95

These tables show an extraordinary rapidity of increase in the value of the real estate in the upper portions of the Island—the Nineteenth Ward being chiefly conspicuous for the advance in its value. This is not entirely, but largely, attributable to the improvements of the Park.*

The other public grounds in the city of New York are the Battery, containing 30 acres; City Hall Park, 10¼ acres; Washington Parade Ground, 9½ acres; Union Square, 4 acres; Stuyvesant Park, 4 acres : Tompkins Square, 10½ acres; Madison Square, 7 acres; St. John's Park, 4 acres; Gramercy Park, 1½ acres :—making a total of 943 acres of ground devoted to park purposes in New York. It may be said to the credit of the Central Park Commissioners, and in fact this may be said with regard to all the different Park Commissioners throughout the country, that although their expenditures have been enormous, they have never been charged with dishonesty.

Eleventh Annual Report of Commissioners of the Central Park.

BALTIMORE.

Druid Hill Park, at Baltimore, was opened October 19, 1860, by a grand celebration, and an address by Mayor Swann. This site is one of the most ancient estates in Maryland, the patent bearing date 1688, and is situated in the northern part of the city, containing 550 acres. The name was suggested by the great number and magnificent oaks which abound everywhere upon it, and was selected on account of the " suitability of the location to the wants of the people, accessibility to the great masses of the community, and its facilities for conversion to the plans and uses of a public park ; also its natural beauty and attractiveness, and the cost of placing it in a condition to meet the demands of the public." *

A large portion of the Park is covered by a primitive forest of oak, hickory, tulip, linden, maple, dogwood, &c. The ground is high and gently undulating, with here and there a deep ravine, in which are found springs and running brooks. It commands a fine view from its height of Chesapeake Bay, Fort McHenry, and the city of Baltimore.

This park has its origin in the prudence and forethought of Mayor Swann, who was impressed with the idea that the city passenger railways should pay something as a compensation for the use of the streets, and, in his address, he says,—"While Baltimore desired a park, and while she was in no condition to impose additional taxes upon her people, it occurred to the friends of this measure that she could do nothing more wise or beneficial, after placing her tariff on an equal footing with her sister cities, to avail herself of the only opportunity likely to secure an adequate bonus to be applied to the purchase of a public park. Accordingly, when the ordinance creating these passenger railways was presented for my approval, I deemed it my duty to insist, as a condition of the franchise, that one-fifth of the gross receipts should go into the treasury as a fund for this purpose."

This was done, and up to December 31, 1868, the sum of $547,546.19 has been received from this source, which has been applied to the payment of the interest of the park bonds, and its improvement. The original cost was $512,193.44 ; this, with the additions, improvements and interest, amounted, as the total cost, December 31, 1868, to $1,302,410.61.†

---

* Mayor Swann's *Dedication Address.*
† *Ninth Annual Report Park Commission.*

Druid Hill Park has been slowly and steadily improved, and will, no doubt, ere long be one of the most delightful resorts in the country. In 1863, Silver Spring was highly ornamented by the liberality of Gerard T. Hopkins; and in 1864, Edmund's Well was adorned by the munificence of John A. Needles. Various works of art, and specimens of natural history, such as swan and deer, have been presented by liberal donors. In 1863, additions were made to this park—among them Mount Vernon Cemetery. Chapman Lake was completed in 1866, and covers sixty-five acres.

Mr. Daniels, who had laid out a number of rural cemeteries, was first employed to adapt this beautiful old private park to public purposes. The purchase and improvement of this ground has enhanced the value of property in its vicinity more than 250 per cent.

Patterson's park was purchased in 1860, for $42,642.50. It is situated in the eastern part of the city, and commands a fine view of the harbor and bay. On it are the remains of a fortification erected for the defence of the city in 1812. It contains thirty-five and one-half acres, six of which are covered by fine trees. The cost, to Dec. 31, 1868, with interest and improvements, was $130,593.78, making the total expenditure for park purposes, by the city of Baltimore, to that time, $1,433,013.30. Both parks have, for the last five years, been under the management of August Faul. Although the expenditures have not been lavish, great improvements have been made, reflecting the highest credit upon the commission for judicious and economic management.

It is said that Mr. Hopkins has donated Clifton Park to the city of Baltimore, for public purposes. This is one of the most elaborate places in the United States. In addition to a fine and costly house, there is nowhere in this country, probably, so large a range of glass, with such diversified grounds, great variety of trees, shrubs, walks, lawns, and large pieces of ornamental water, containing numerous islands, planted with masses of rhododendrons and evergreen shrubs, connected by tasteful and appropriate bridges.

BROOKLYN.

Prospect Park, Brooklyn, although of more recent origin, bids fair to become a formidable rival to the Central Park of New York, as the ground in some respects is better adapted for the purpose. The land had been selected for some time prior to the final purchase, in 1864. It was not until 1866, that much improvement was made, when those accomplished landscape gardeners, Olmsted and

Vaux, were placed in charge. The design is truly beautiful, and if carried out as commenced, with the park-way, will make Prospect Park and its vicinity one of the loveliest spots in this country.

Since 1866, 250 acres of the 550, of which it is composed, have been under treatment, and 19,000 feet in length of carriage, and 17,000 feet of walk completed, and over 100,000 trees and shrubs set out; and since October 20, 1866, when carriages were first admitted, it has become quite a favorite resort.

The land originally cost the city June 15, 1864,...............$1,357,606.27
First addition, Feb. 4, 1866,.................................... 158,558.41
Second addition, May 27, 1867,................................ 752,745.02

Total cost of land,......................................$2,268,909.70
Cost of improvements to Dec. 31, 1867,............ .... 1,169,604.70

Total cost, ...$3,438,514.40

The interest, payable semi-annually, is raised by annual tax on the First, Twelfth and the Twentieth Wards of the city. Soon after work commenced in the park, the price of lots rose rapidly in the neighborhood, and recent sales show increasing value. The assessed value of the real estate in the Eight Ward, exclusive of the amount assessed for buildings, has increased over 30 per cent. during the last year, while the increased value of the real estate of the Eight and Ninth Wards, being the two wards immediately contiguous to the park, has for the same time, amounted to nearly two-thirds of the increased value of the entire city. A similar increase from the same cause, though not to the same extent, is perceptible in the Twentieth Ward, which comes next in contiguity to the park, and doubtless an increase exists in several of the other wards, particularly the Tenth.

The records of the Board of City Assessors show that the assessed value of real estate in the year 1864 was:

In the Eighth Ward,...............................$4,913,274
In the Ninth Ward,......................... 7,966,471
In the Twentieth Ward, ... 7,069,650

Total, ... $19,949,395
The same record for the year 1867 shows:
In the Eighth Ward,...........................$ 7,983,200
In the Ninth Ward,............................... 10,743,797
In the Twentieth Ward,.......................... 8,705,090

Total in three wards,.......... .... $27,432,087
Increased in valuation since active operations
commenced in parks,............................ $7,482,692

The additional tax which was raised from this increased valuation for the year 1867, was $280,692, while the annual interest on the whole park debt, as it now stands, is $229,219, showing an annual increase of revenue to the city, from three wards alone, of $51,473. *

* *Eighth Annual Report of Commissioners of Prospect Park.*

At the request of the Common Council, the Legislature placed four of the smaller parks under the charge of the Board of Prospect Park, viz., the Carroll, City, Washington (thirty acres), and City Hall parks. In the latter are to be placed the remains of the Prison-ship martyrs. Washington Park was laid out in 1848, and although plans have been made for its improvement, it has been proposed to lay it out in lots, and sell them for the benefit of the city. There is a cemetery included in Prospect Park, from which the bodies are, however, to be removed.

SAVANNAH, NEW ORLEANS, SAN FRANCISCO, DETROIT, AND CLEVELAND.

Savannah has a great many small public squares, some of which are laid out with much taste, and many of the streets are lined with the Pride of China trees, presenting a beautiful and unique aspect. New Orleans has its Jackson Square, formerly the *Place d' Armes*, which was laid out at the foundation of the city, and which has recently been much improved. In it is the equestrian statue of Gen. Jackson, by Clark Mills. Upon the granite block whereon it stands, Gen. Butler, while in the military occupation of the city, caused to be engraved, "The Union, it must be preserved." La Fayette Square, in another portion of the city, is pleasantly laid out. There are also several smaller squares. Owing to the peculiar manner in which Detroit is laid out, there are many pieces of ground of different sizes and shapes, intended for the public use. Some of them are now being improved, and when completed will add much to the appearance and beauty of that city. San Francisco has twelve squares, but the Plaza, or Portsmouth Square, is the only one improved. Cleveland has a fine public square, ornamented with a statue of Perry. Mr. Nicholson proposes to give to this city, for the purposes of a public park, from two hundred to two hundred and fifty acres of ground, lying on both sides of Rock river, provided the city will expend in its improvement, the sum of $50,000 per year for ten years.

CINCINNATI.

Until recently, Cincinnati has had no place that could be called a park. The first effort in supplying this want was the conversion of an old cemetery into Washington Park, containing four and a half acres, almost in the heart of the city; and it looks very prettily, with its lake, fountains, walks, slopes, and venerable trees. The next step was to form Lincoln Park, first called West-End Park, containing seven acres, with its large, handsome lake, and beautiful green island, and which was a great improvement to the West End. Hopkins, containing one and a half acres, and the City Park, one and a fourth acres, are within the built-up parts of the city.

It was not until the water supply question was agitated, and the necessity for a new reservoir of fair capacity became imperative, that the idea of combining a large park and reservoir became popular, four years ago. A portion of the high grounds boldly overlooking the Ohio river, in the eastern part of the city, was selected, known as Longworth's Garden of Eden, as the proper location for the reservoir, to give sufficient head to the water supply. Combined with this advantage was another—that nature had so formed the ground as to leave it susceptible of easy landscape improvement. It contains 156 acres, 14 of which will be covered by water. There are at this time over three miles of avenues laid out, two of which are nearly graded, so that early in the spring the broken stone and gravel can be put on, forming one of the most delightful drives in the vicinity of the city. The grades of all the avenues are very easy, most of them being scarcely perceptible. Nearly the whole ground will be laid off in landscape, and the reservoir adding to the beauties of the scenery, will form a very conspicuous feature. There is no stiff outline or geometrical form to the boundaries of the reservoir, the water forming its own outline by the natural slopes of the hills. There is no point at which a view of the entire lake can be seen, some portions of its surface being lost in the meanderings of its course.

The ground has been leased by the city, and whenever the City should wish to purchase, it can do so, for the sum of $3,000 per acre, but until then it is to pay an annual rent on the above amount at the rate of six per cent. per annum. Work was commenced in May 1867, and up to this time $245,000 have been expended. The improvement is expected to cost $1,400,000. *

ST. LOUIS.

In St. Louis, the subject of public parks has occupied much attention for the past few years, the same diversity of opinion and interest existing as in our city. The city was the owner, in 1866, of 287 acres of land, distributed in various parks, places, and squares throughout the city. In the same year the Mayor recommended the

* Dr. Wm. Clendenin, Health Officer, Cincinnati.

passage of an ordinance authorizing the City Cemetery to be declared a public **park,** and the purchase of the following additions, so as to increase the City Cemetery to $35\frac{35}{100}$ acres, Lafayette Park to $47\frac{94}{100}$ acres, St. Louis Place to $35\frac{18}{100}$ acres, and Hyde Park to $20\frac{70}{100}$ acres; also, the purchase of fifty acres outside of the city limits. This, I believe, was not done. The following are the names, locality, and area of the parks :—

NAMES.	LOCALITY.	AREA.
Carondelet Park......	N. Dacotah street. E. Michigan avenue.	$3\frac{17}{100}$ acres.
Laclede Park.........	N. Gasconade street. E. Iowa avenue.	$3\frac{17}{100}$ "
Gravois Park.........	Potomac street and Kansas avenue...	$8\frac{252}{1000}$ "
Lafayette Park......	Park avenue and Mississippi avenue..	$29\frac{956}{1000}$ "
Washington Square..	Market and 12th streets.............	6 "
Missouri Park........	St. Charles and 13th streets.........	$3\frac{346}{1000}$ "
Carr Square..........	Carr and E. 16th streets.............	$2\frac{607}{1000}$ "
Jackson Place........	Jackson alley and 11th street........	$1\frac{622}{1000}$ "
Clinton Place........	Clinton alley and 11th street........	$1\frac{622}{1000}$ "
Marion Place	Marion alley and 11th street..:.....	$1\frac{622}{1000}$ "
St. Louis Place......	Herbert and 17th streets.............	$15\frac{303}{1000}$ "
Hyde Park..........	Bremen avenue and 12th street......	$11\frac{833}{1000}$ "
Exchange Square.....	Warren street and Wharf............	$15\frac{18}{100}$ "
Tower Grove Park ...	Magnolia and Grand avenue........	$276\frac{76}{100}$ "
Benton Park........	Arsenal st. & McHose & English Cave.	$15\frac{50}{100}$ "

Mr. Henry Shaw several years ago offered to donate to the city of St. Louis 200 acres, on condition that a certain strip surrounding the tract be reserved by him and sold for residences, the proceeds to constitute a part of the endowment of his "Botanical Garden." On March 9, 1867, an act was passed by the Legislature of Missouri creating, and providing for the government of Tower-Grove Park; and on July 3, 1868, the City Council passed an ordinance to raise the requisite funds, for carrying out the provisions of the act. Owing to the fact that provision is made in the act creating the park for its improvement, Mr. Shaw donated 76 acres more than he originally intended. He is constituted a Commissioner during his life, and he also appoints the remaining four Commissioners. The grounds are partially improved, and with the arboretum, botanical garden, &c., constitute one of the most liberal gifts ever made by a private gentleman for the public benefit. I am informed that the necessary funds have been raised for its improvement, and that as soon as possible work will be commenced.*

CHICAGO.

Coming now to Chicago we find her public grounds distributed as follows : in the North Division is Lincoln Park, containing about 50 acres, 25 of which may be said to be improved, whereon the sum of $60,000 has been very judiciously expended during the last three years, making it a truly beautiful place. With the lake and the character of the ground, there is here afforded a fine opportunity for landscape gardening. Many trees have been set out, and two and a half miles of carriage drives, and about the same length of graded walks, have been constructed. Unfortunately the carriage drives are not wide enough. Several picturesque lakes are also found in it. Washington Park is also in the North Division, situated between North Dearborn and North Clark streets, and Washington and Lafayette places. It contains $2\frac{2}{10}$ acres, upon which a few trees have been planted, and improved by two concrete walks running through it, and is enclosed by a common fence. Lake Park, is a tract lying along the lake in front of Michigan avenue, extending from Randolph street to Park Place, and when filled will contain about 40 acres. Dearborn Park is between Washington and Randolph streets, fronting on Michigan avenue, containing $1\frac{43}{100}$ acres, and is surrounded by an iron railing with a few stunted trees scattered here and there, together with an occasional evergreen. The attempts at improvement of this piece of ground have been singularly abortive, and in a sanitary point of view much more benefit can be derived by the sale of this property for business purposes, and the application of the proceeds to the purchase of grounds elsewhere,—as for instance in the 5th Ward between 26th and 31st streets. The Court House Square contains $2\frac{8}{10}$ acres, but with the extension of the public buildings the area which will be left for decoration will be insignificant. Several unsuccessful attempts have been made to improve this square. Ellis Park has an area of about 3 acres, and is situated near the Douglas Monument, and is covered by a few forest trees. Union Park on the West Side contains 17 acres whose improvements have cost the sum of $42,584.74. The attempt at landscape gardening in this park has been unfortunate, as the extent and character of the

* Dr. P. V. Schenck, Health Officer, St. Louis.

ground is such that it will not admit of anything of the kind. Jefferson Park containing $5\frac{4}{10}$ acres, is situated between Monroe and Adams streets, on the north and south, and Rucker and Loomis streets east and west, and is surrounded by a wooden fence, and has been laid out in walks, and a few trees have been planted in and around it. The same may be said of the Vernon Park, which contains four acres. Wicker Park, is a projected one in the extreme north-western part of the city. The whole area within the city, devoted to park purposes, amounts to $125\frac{93}{100}$ acres, of which only one-third has been improved, and upon the improvements about $105,000 have been expended. *

I have thus passed in review the history of parks and public grounds, from the earliest period to the present time. Apart from considerations of sanitary economy, of which I shall treat hereafter, it will be seen that public parks may be regarded as an unerring index of the advance of a people in civilization and refinement. They form an attractive feature in the surroundings of any great city, and constitute, even, the peculiar charm of many a country village. From the foregoing it will be seen how much has been accomplished elsewhere, and how little here. This is owing, no doubt, to the rapidity with which Chicago has sprung up. But it is singular, that with all her characteristic business energy and forethought, she has so far neglected to secure ample grounds for park purposes; but the time has now arrived when it becomes necessary to act, and act in a manner that will not leave her behind, as compared with other cities, in those arts which embellish and render cities attractive as places of abode; in other words, we want, not alone a place for business, but also one in which we can live.

* In this connection, it may not be out of place to call attention to the *suburban village* at Riverside, located in a bend of the Aux Plaines River, nine miles south-west from the business center of Chicago, and six miles west of the city limits. It is a private enterprise, and is intended as a resident park, comprising an area of 1,600 acres, which has been laid out, and is now being improved, under the direction of Olmsted and Vaux, formerly architects and landscape gardeners of the Central Park, New York, and now of the Prospect Park, Brooklyn. The greater portion of the ground is admirably adapted for this purpose, being about twenty feet above the river, making it easily susceptible of good drainage, while the banks of the river and the more elevated portions of the ground are covered with groves of thrifty trees, consisting of oaks, elms, hickories, walnuts, lindens, and ashes. Here are to be combined the comforts of the city, in the way of gas, water, drainage, with all the beauties of landscape gardening ; and I have no doubt, judging from the report of the architects to the owners, and the work already accomplished, that it will be made one of the finest suburban parks in the country, and one of the most pleasant and healthful places of residence in the neighborhood of this city. To facilitate access, it is also intended to connect this park with the city by a broad and well improved avenue, lined with trees. If it were for nothing else, this enterprise cannot be too strongly commended, on account of the trees that are to be planted along this avenue, which, in the course of time, will exercise a vast influence in moderating the extremes of our climate, and go far to protect the city from the injurious effects of the south-west wind at certain seasons of the year. As the approaches to the city in that direction are an open waste, and exceedingly uninteresting, and, at times, positively dreary and difficult, owing to character of the roads, Riverside and the avenue will soon cause the improvement of the intervening space, and thus obviate this objection.

HOW FAR MAN CAN MODIFY CLIMATE.

Marsh, in his work on "Man and Nature," says: "The influence of man in changing the climate and the physical condition of a country needs no argument to substantiate." Withdraw man, and you remove the disturber of all laws. People must be "awakened to the necessity of restoring the disturbed harmonies of nature, where well-balanced influences are so propitious to all her organic offspring, of repaying to our great mother the debt which the prodigality and thriftlessness of former generations have imposed upon their successors—thus fulfilling the command of religion and of practical wisdom, to use this world as not abusing it." He further says: "I am satisfied that we can become the architects of our own abiding place, as it is well known how the mode of our physical, moral, and intellectual being is affected by the character of the home Providence has appointed, and we have fashioned for our material habitation."

Such is undoubtedly the case, and it becomes our duty to restore, as far as possible, this harmony, which is destroyed by the accumulation of such a mass of human beings, as are now congregated in and around this city. The collection of many people in a small space, no matter for what purpose, is unnatural and artificial. It is therefore necessary, in order to prevent the ill effects of such accumulations, to resort to artificial means to equalize the disturbing agencies. Will we then intelligently use what knowledge we have, and avert the result, or fold our hands, and depend upon blind chance, bearing in mind, however, that

"Death lives where power lives unused."

In the discussion of the questions involved, in order to arrive at satisfactory results, it is necessary to examine into all its aspects and relations systematically; and when conclusions are arrived at, their application must be made in like manner, in order to produce the desired result.

"Science," says Whewell, "is that precise and comprehensive kind of knowledge which results from the application to facts, which are sufficiently numerous, of conceptions clear and distinct in themselves, and so suited to the facts as to produce an exact and uniform accordance; and the construction of science is a process which comprises methods of observation, methods of obtaining clear ideas, and methods of induction."* "Science," says Lord Bacon, evidently following the definition of Pliny, "is the interpretation of nature,"

---

* Bain on the *Senses and the Intellect*

" a comparison," says Bain, "that transfixes the mind with the idea of observing, recording, and explaining the facts of the world."

This definition I shall apply to sanitary science, in connection with public parks, and, as best I can, explain general laws and draw deductions from the facts within my reach, with regard to the climate, topography, and diseases of this locality. Although some of the facts collected during 1866, and the first half of 1867, are not as full nor as accurate as those collected since, still they are sufficiently so to indicate the general laws governing and controlling them.

VEGETABLE PHYSIOLOGY.

In order to appreciate the important part that the vegetable kingdom performs in the economy of nature, and particularly its effects upon animal life, it will be necessary to call attention to the elementary composition of plants, the nature of the food by which they are nourished, the sources from which this food is derived, and the transformation it undergoes in their system. In the process of digestion or assimilation is found the nature of vegetation, as in this process alone mineral and unorganized matter is converted into the tissues of plants and other forms of organized matter, the vegetable kingdom occupying a position between the mineral and the animal kingdoms. In living bodies there is a state of internal activity and unceasing change—particles which have served their turn being continually thrown out of the system as new ones are brought in, thus constantly undergoing decomposition and recomposition. Plants are organized beings that live directly upon the mineral kingdom—and upon the surrounding earth and air, and, as a necessary result of assimilating their organic food,they decompose carbonic acid, and restore its oxygen to the atmosphere. Animals in respiration, continually recompose carbonic acid at the expense of the oxygen of the atmosphere and the carbon of plants. Plants absorb their food entirely in a liquid or gaseous form, by imbibition, according to the law of endosmosis, through the walls of the cells that form the surface—as when liquids of unequal density are separated by a permeable membrane, the lighter liquid or the weaker solution will flow into the denser or stronger with a force proportioned to the difference in density ; but at the same time a smaller portion of the denser liquid will flow out into the weaker, which process is called exosmosis.

The fluid absorbed by the roots, is thus carried from cell to cell, rising principally in the wood, and is attracted to the leaves, or other parts of the plants exposed to sun and light, by the exhalation which takes place from them, and the consequent inspiration of the sap.   Here the crude sap is exposed to sun and light, and assimilated and converted into organizable matter.   Carbon, hydrogen, oxygen, and nitrogen, are indispensable to vegetation, and make up at least from 88 to 90 per cent. of every vegetable substance ; the proper vegetable structure, however, is only composed of carbon, hydrogen, and oxygen.

Plants also receive nitrogen in the form of ammonia, which is always produced when any animal, and almost when any vegetable substance decays, and which, being very volatile, continually rises into the air from these and other sources.   Ammonia is soluble and is greedily absorbed by aqueous vapor, and is brought to the ground by rain and snow.   The carbon of plants is derived wholly from the carbonic acid of the atmosphere, and it makes up $\frac{1}{3200}$ of its bulk, from which it is directly absorbed by the leaves.   It may then be said that the atmosphere contains all the essentials to plant growth, viz., water in a state of vapor, which is not only food itself as it supplies oxygen and hydrogen, but is likewise the vehicle of the others, carrying to the roots what it has gathered from the air, namely, the requisite supplies of nitrogen, either as such, or in the form of ammonia, and of carbon in the form of carbonic acid.

In fact, all of the essential elements of plants or proper food may be absorbed by the leaves directly from the air, and no doubt most plants take in a great part of their food in this way as drooping foliage may be revived by sprinkling with water, or exposure to a damp atmosphere.

Air plants live on the atmosphere, and a branch of the common "Live Forever" will grow when pinned to a dry and bare wall. All leafy plants derive their carbonic acid from the air, and many, as has already been stated, derive their whole food from the air or part of it.   It is found, that when a current of carbonic acid is made to traverse a glass globe containing a leafy plant exposed to full sunshine, some carbonic acid disappears, and an equal bulk of oxygen gas supplies its place.   Now since carbonic acid gas contains just its own bulk of oxygen, it is evident that what has thus been decomposed in the leaves has returned all its oxygen to the air.

Although plants may derive their food from the air, they receive it mainly through the roots. The *aqueous vapor*, condensed into rain or dew, and bringing with it to the ground a portion of carbonic acid and of nitrogen or ammonia, &c., supplies the proper food of the plant to the rootlets, and imbibed by these it is conveyed through the stem and into the leaves where the superfluous water is restored to the atmosphere by exhalation, while the residue is converted into the proper nourishment and substance of the vegetable.

The water exhaled may be again absorbed by the roots laden with a new supply of the other elements from the air, again exhaled and so on, as illustrated by cultivated plants in Ward's case, where plants are seen to flourish for a long time with a limited supply of water, every particle of which (excepting the small portion actually consumed by the plants,) must repeatedly pass through this circulation ; and here is exhibited the actual relations of water, &c., to vegetation on a large scale in nature, where the water is alternately and repeatedly raised by evaporation and recondensed t o such an extent that what actually falls in rain is estimated to be evaporated and rained down on an average ten or fifteen times a year. In this way the atmosphere is repeatedly purified by the rain, and those vapors washed out, which else by their accumulations, would prove injurious to man and animals, and are conveyed to the roots of plants which they are especially adapted to nourish.

During intensely hot weather the effect of rain is apparent, and the common saying "We have had a refreshing shower," is appreciated by all. A shower of rain has been known frequently to stop epidemics, particularly of cholera.

The lower order of plants, such as the Lichens, Mosses, Ferns, &c., which grow entirely at the expense of the air and are generally found in damp and shady places, gradually form a soil or vegetable mould during their life, which is increased by their decay, while the successive generations live more vigorously upon this inheritance, being supported partly by what they draw from the air and partly from the ancestral accumulations of vegetable mould. It is in this way that, what are called the useless plants create a soil which will in time support the higher plants of immediate importance to man and other mammalia, but which could never grow and perfect their fruits if left like their humble predecessors to derive an unaided subsistance directly from the inorganic mould. The harmony of nature is such that it cannot be disturbed. The greater part of

Fungi live upon decaying organic matter, and have not the power
of forming organizable products from inorganic material.

We now come to that part of vegetable physiology in which we
are most interested. Under the influence of light, takes place the
chemical decomposition of one or more substances in the sap,
liberating the oxygen at the ordinary temperature of the air,
and transforming the mineral, inorganic food into organic matter—
the organized substance of living plants and animals. The chief
material given back to the air in this process is oxygen gas, that
element of our atmosphere which renders it fit for the breathing and
life of animals. That the foliage of plants in sunshine is continually
yielding oxygen to the surrounding air has been known since the
days of Ingenloup and Priestly. By exposing a few freshly-
gathered leaves to the sunshine, in a glass vessel filled with water,
air-bubbles will presently arise but cease to appear when placed in
the dark.

There is no doubt but that all leafy plants obtain part of their carbonic acid from the air, for when a current of carbonic acid gas is
made slowly to traverse a glass globe containing a leafy plant exposed
to full sunshine, some carbonic acid disappears, and an equal bulk of
oxygen gas supplies its place. Carbonic acid gas contains just its
own bulk of oxygen. It is evident that what has thus been decomposed in the leaves, has returned all its oxygen to the air. Plants,
therefore, take carbonic acid, directly or indirectly ; they retain its
carbon, and give back its oxygen.

Generally speaking, the plants may be said to be in a passive or
or state of rest at night, sometimes even throwing out carbonic acid
and consuming oxygen, and this is undoubtedly the reason why more
deaths occur at night, and the fatality incident to epidemics is
greatest.

In fact vegetation is the only operation in nature which gives to
the air free oxygen which is indispensable to animal life, as all
animals consume oxygen at every moment of their life, giving to the
air carbonic acid in its room, and when dead their bodies consume a
further portion in decomposition, such being the case also with
vegetables. While animals consume the oxygen of the air, and give
back carbonic acid which is injurious to their life, this carbonic acid
is the principle element of the food of vegetables, is consumed and
decomposed by them, and its oxygen returned for the use of animals.
Hence the perfect adaptation of the two great kingdoms of living

beings to each other; each removing from the atmosphere which would be noxious to the other—each yielding to the atmosphere what is essential to the continued existence of the other.* Little does man think how dependent he is upon vegetation, for while the vegetable kingdom is entirely independent, and might have existed alone, yet it is absolutely essential to the life of man.†

AQUATIC VEGETATION.

The remarks thus far made, generally apply to the vegetable kingdom, and have mainly had reference to the higher orders of plants. I now propose to advert to the lower orders which occur in water, both fresh and salt, and play the same part in the economy of nature, as those found on land. They have been found in countless myriads in the depths of the ocean, far down as the plummet has yet sounded, and in fact, may be said to be found in every climate under one phase or another.‡ The sea teems with animal life, and without

---

* Gray's *Structural Botany.*

† It has been found by experiment that plants will thrive in air containing more carbonic acid than that usually found in the atmosphere when exposed to a strong sun-light, or in climates where the solar light is not much obscured by clouds. The floating islands which are constantly being found in the lake of Solfatara, in Italy, according to Sir Humphrey Davy, exhibit a striking example of cryptogamic vegetation in an atmosphere impregnated with carbonic acid. These islands consist chiefly of confervæ and other simple cellular plants, which are copiously supplied with nutriment by carbonic acid that is constantly escaping from the bottom of the lake, with a violence that gives to the water an appearance of ebullition. Dr. Schleiden, *Weigman's Archives*, 1838, mentions that the vegetation around the springs in the valley of Gottingen, which abound in carbonic acid, is very rich and luxuriant; appearing several weeks earlier in spring, and continuing much later in autumn, than at other spots in the same district. Humboldt says that "exhalations of carbonic acid (mofettes) are, even in our days, to be considered as the most important gaseous emanations, with respect to their number and the amount of their effusion. We see in Germany, in the deep valleys of Eifel, in the neighborhood of Lake Laach, in the crater-like valley of the Wehr of Western Bohemia, exhalations of carbonic acid gas manifest themselves as the last efforts of volcanic activity, in or near the foci of an earlier world. In these earlier periods, when a higher terrestrial temperature existed, and when a great number of fissures remained unfilled, the processes we have described acted more powerfully, and carbonic acid and hot steam were mixed in larger quantities in the atmosphere, from whence it follows, as Adolph Brongniart has ingeniously shown, (in the *Annales des Sciences Naturelles*,) that the primitive vegetable world must have exhibited, almost everywhere, and independently of geographical position, the most luxurious abundance and the fullest development of organism. In these constantly warm and damp atmospheric strata, saturated with carbonic acid, vegetation must have attained a degree of vital activity, and derived the superabundance of nutrition necessary to furnish material for the formation of the beds of lignite, (coal,) constituting the inexhaustible means on which are based the physcial power and prosperity of nations." * * *
"That portion of the carbon which was not taken up by the alkaline earths, but remained mixed with the atmosphere as carbonic acid, was gradually consumed by the vegetation of the earlier stages of the world, so that the atmosphere, after being purified by the processes of vegetable life, only retained the small quantity which it now possesses, and which is not injurious to the present organization of animal life."—*Cosmos.* Daubney, in his work on "Volcanoes," says, speaking of the Lake of Laach, that "the thickness of the vegetation on the sides of its crater-like basin, renders it difficult to discover the nature of the subjacent rock." The same writer, in his "Report to the British Association," for 1849, of experiments made by him, confirms, to a great extent, the ingenious hypothesis of M. Brongniart.

‡ Although the surface of the ocean is less rich in living forms than that of continents, it is not improbable that on a farther investigation of its depths, its interior may be found to possess a greater richness of organic life than any other portion of our planet. Charles Darwin, in the agreeable narrative of his extensive voyages, justly remarks that our forests do not conceal so many animals as the low, woody regions of the ocean, where the sea-weed rooted to the bottom of the shoals, and the several branches of foci loosened by the force of the waves and currents, and swimming free, unfold their delicate foliage, upborne by air cells.—*Cosmos.*

these, vegetable forms they could not live.* They keep the water pure, and yield oxygen to the atmosphere. In every pool and stagnant ditch, under the influence of heat, algæ are quickly produced, forming the green scum over them, which instead of being injurious, are beneficial, and emit oxygen in the shape of beads that can be seen on any sunny day. It is only after the pool is dried, and these confervæ are wafted away by the wind, that places of this character become injurious. The amount of benefit derived from these apparently insignificant plants, is great when we take into account the many extensive surfaces of water dispersed over the world, which are thus kept pure, and made subservient to a healthy state of the atmosphere. It is not only vast, but part of the harmonious whole, and worthy of Him who has appointed even to the meanest of His creatures, something to do for the good of His creation ;† and well may it be said—

> "Call us not weeds, we are the flowers of the sea."

INFLUENCE OF VEGETATION, PARTICULARLY TREES, UPON HEALTH.

Having thus shown the actions and reactions which take place between animal and vegetable life, and how dependent the former is upon the latter, we propose to call attention to a series of facts, gathered from different sources, which illustrate in a marked degree, the application of these principles, clearly proving that the infection and diffusion of malaria or noxious emanations are arrested by trees, whose structure and canopy of foliage act in a three-fold capacity ; —first as a barrier to break the flow, second as an absorbent of those emanations, and third as eliminators of oxygen.

Lancisi cites a number of facts showing the protection afforded by belts of trees against the effects of malaria, and the danger resulting from their removal. He calls attention to the fact that, in former days, there existed on the south side of Rome a thick forest which extended from Frascati and Albano to the Tiber, and protected the southern portion of the city and the neighboring district from the baneful influence of the effluvia of the Pontine Marshes. This

---

* "The parlor aquarium has taught even those to whom it is but an amusing toy, that the balance of animal and vegetable life must be preserved, and that excess of either is fatal to the other, in the artificial tank as well as in natural water. A few years ago, the water of the Cochituate Aqueduct, at Boston, became so offensive in smell and taste, as to be quite unfit for use. Scientific investigation found the cause in the scrupulous care with which aquatic vegetation had been excluded from the reservoir, and the consequent death and decay of the animalculæ which could not be shut out nor live in the water without the the vegetable element."—*Man and Nature:* Marsh.

† *Contributions to the History of Marine Algæ of North America:* Harvey.

rampart has since been removed, and the country has become proverbial for its unhealthiness.*

Lancisi did not for a moment doubt the utility of these belts, and expresses the opinion that the consecration by the Ancients of woods and groves had no other motive than guarding, through their means, against the diffusion of the febriferous poison. Among the Romans, the advantage of such barriers had long been recognized. Trees were planted in rows and masses to guard against the diffusion of malaria. The practice was enforced by law, and recorded in the Roman tablets. This law, which was reported by Cicero,—" Lucos in agris habinto,"—evidently had reference much more to the advantage in question than for the purposes for which trees are usually planted. In order to insure their safety, such collections of trees were placed under the protection of some divinity, or under the responsibility of the Roman Consuls.

Bapt. Donus, in his work " On the means insuring Salubrity to the Soil of the Roman States," recommends the planting of pine and other trees between Rome and the Pontine Marshes, to intercept the miasmata wafted from there by the south-west winds. At Velletri, as also at Campo-Salino, the destruction of belts of woods was followed by the prevalence of fever.†

Dr. Lewis, in his Medical History of Alabama, says, " Mr. P. E. had negro-quarters situated on the first prairie elevation above the low lands of a small creek, the fourth of a mile from the houses. The belt of low ground frequently overflowed, causing water to remain in holes over its entire breadth, in the subsidence of the stream ; but it was well shaded by a dense foliage, the plantation lying on the prairie in the rear of the cabins. In the winter of 1842 and 1843 the trees between the houses and creek were cleared away, and up to that time, some eight or ten years, the negroes living in this quarter had enjoyed uninterrupted health—a case of fever scarcely occurring. During the summer of 1843, the first after the forest had been cleared away, fever prevailed among the negroes with great violence, continuing until frost. The negro-quarters were afterwards removed to the opposite side of the creek, about the same distance from it, but with an intervening growth of timber, and no fever has occurred on the place since." ‡

---

* La Roche, on *Pneumonia and Malaria.*
† De Restituenda Salubritate Agri Romani, 1667.
‡ New Orleans *Journal.*

"Whole families," says Mr. Bartlett, "have resided near the Pontine Marshes, and, by the intenvention of shrubs and trees, have escaped for years the noxious effects of the mephitic vapors which these putrid waters engender."* Dr. Hosack states that a family in New Jersey was attacked with fever in consequence of cutting down a wood that separated them from a morass in the neighborhood. Before the operation they had been healthy.† "Army physicians, therefore, recommend," says Dr. Wilson Philip, "having a wood, if possible, between marshy grounds and an encampment."‡ Rigault de Lisle calls attention to the fact that, upon Mount Argental, above the village of St. Stephano, there is a convent which has lost all the reputation for salubrity which it once enjoyed, since the lofty trees, by which it was surrounded, have been cut down. "I have been informed," he adds, "by persons worthy of credit, that in consequence of the felling of the wood before Asterna, near the Pontine Marshes. Veletri was visited for three successive years by diseases which made much greater havoc than usual throughout the whole country, and penetrated to many places which they had not previously been accustomed to reach. Rigault de Lisle cites other cases, and refers to Volney, who states that Beyroot, formerly very unhealthy, has ceased to be so since the Emir Fakr-el-din planted a wood of fir-trees, which still exist, a league below the town.

By Pliny and others, among the Ancients, it was supposed that trees absorb the exhalations extricated from insalubrious places, and that the beneficial effects obtained from woods are to be accounted for in this way much more than the obstacles they offer to the diffusion of these exhalations. This opinion has, to a certain extent, received the sanction of Thouvenelle, Copland, and other modern writers; and it is is undoubtedly correct, as the results of certain experiments made long ago, and repeated more recently, prove. Dr. Lewis, of Mobile, says, "It is the received opinion that living vegetation protects the human system from the deleterious effects of malaria; and, reasoning by analogy, it would appear that experiments made by scientific men have satisfactorily explained the mutual dependence of the animal kingdoms on each other for support. It has been ascertained that if air, rendered pernicious by respiration, be confined in a bottle, into which some green plant has been intro-

---

* Thompson's *Annals.*
† *Practice of Medicine.*
‡ *Treatise on Feb. Dis.*

duced, and exposed to the action of the sun, the carbonic acid will be absorbed, and the air restored to its original condition. The putrefaction of animal matter, and the decomposition of vegetable substances, would cause a sufficiency of carbonic acid vapor, when united with atmospheric air, to destroy every living being, were it not for this wise provision of nature. This gas, which is poisonous to the human as well as animal species, is a source of nutriment to every variety of plants; and thus, it would appear, exercises a benign influence in protecting man from the deleterious effects of poisonous vapors. And if the effect is obtained, so far as regards one species of poisonous vapor, it may be equally so in reference to that giving rise to fever." *

Dr. Cartwright ascribes to the *Jussiœa grandiflora*, a plant found in great abundance in marshy or swampy places in the Southern States, particularly in certain regions of Louisiana, which present the usual characteristic malarial surfaces, the cause of their exemption from fever.† Aquatic plants and those found in swampy or marshy soils while growing, exhale a large quantity of oxygen; but when they have their growth, this action ceases and those regions become unhealthy. It was at one time supposed that no ozone could be found in swamps; but I have discovered its presence in June, near the surface of the water of a lake in which the Chara were growing abundantly, but could not detect it in the same place in September. It has also been ascertained that fish are healthier and thrive better in water where aquatic plants are found than where they are absent.

A distinguished natural philosopher, Changeux, inferred from the results of his experiments, that the action of trees in producing the effects under consideration, is two-fold. "Plants," he says, "whether odoriferous or inodorous, give issue to emanations which, when mixed with poisonous vapors exhaling from marshy or damp soils, neutralize their pernicious influence. But the former exercise a greater effect through means of the neutralizing process than by the power of absorption just mentioned, their emanations mixing with the air we breathe and correcting its deleterious properties by virtue of the particular qualities with which they are endowed. The second class—the inodoriferous—on the other hand, act more evidently through means of their power of absorption than of the

---

* *Medical History of Alabama.*
† *Western Medical Journal.*

neutralizing property of their emanation, and remove from the air the vapors by which it is contaminated."*

M. Carriere, in a work on the climate of Italy, adopts the views of Chevreul and Fontana, in relation to the febrific poison through means of the action of organic matter on the sulphates contained in the earth, or in water with the aid of the oxygen derived from the former. The leaves of plants and of trees, as well as the green substances that cover the soil, are all inexhaustible sources of oxygen, which is so important to sustain life and preserve health. "Hence," he says, "to cover the fields, the edges of marshes and the whole extent of the soil with an abundant vegetation, is equal to placing on the surface of unhealthy regions a reparative apparatus of the greatest power. Trees, therefore, must have a large share in the amelioration of the country, in consequence of the quantity of leaves they furnish."†

Others have supposed, before vegetable physiology was as well understood as at this time, that malaria was collected by plants, particularly those of a dense and entangling foliage, and was disengaged in cutting them down or rooting them up, thus exciting fevers and disease. Dr. Ferguson, calling attention to the attraction of marsh poison for, or rather its adherence to, lofty umbrageous trees, says that "this is so much the case that it can with difficulty be separated from them; and that in the territory of Guiana particularly, where these trees abound, it is wonderful to see how near to leeward of the most pestiferous marshes the settlers, provided they have this security, will venture—and that with comparative impunity—to place their habitations. The town of New Amsterdam, Berbice, situated within musket shot to leeward of a swamp extremely offensive at a certain stage of dryness, owes evidently its exemption from fever to this cause." "A still better instance of the same, and with the same results, may be seen at Paramaribo, the capital of Surinam, when the trade-wind, that regularly ventilates the town and renders it habitable, blows over a swamp within a mile of the town, which, fortunately for the inhabitants, is covered with the same description of trees."‡

"It has been observed," says Becqueral, "that humid air, charged with miasmata, is deprived of them in passing through

---

* *Journal de Physique.*
† *Le Climat de l'Italie.*
‡ *Marsh Poison.*

the forest. Rigaud de Lisle observed localities in Italy where the interposition of a screen of trees preserved everything beyond it, while the unprotected grounds were subject to fevers."* The belief that rows of trees afford an important protection against malarious influences is very general among Italians best qualified by intelligence and professional experience, to judge upon the subject. The commissioners appointed to report on the measures to be adopted for the improvement of the Tuscan Maremme advised the planting of three or four rows of poplars, in such directions as to obstruct the currents of air from malarious localities, and thus intercept a great proportion of the pernicious exhalations." † Lieutenant Maury believed that a few rows of sun-flowers, planted between the Washington Observatory and the marshy banks of the Potomac, had saved the inmates of that establishment from the intermittent fever, to which they had been formerly liable. These experiments have been repeated in Italy. Large plantations of sun-flowers have been made upon the alluvial deposits of the Oglio, above its entrance into the lake of Iseo, near Pisogne, and it is said with beneficial effects. ‡

"In Southern Burmah the inhabitants place their houses under trees with the best effect, and it was a rule with the Romans to encamp their men under trees in all hot countries." §

Many more instances of a like character might be adduced that have occurred in this country, particularly in the West. In the settlement of all new countries much sickness follows, owing to the destruction of the trees and the upturning of the vegetable mould which has for ages been collecting and lying dormant, and thus exposed by the influence of heat and light to decomposition. The " balance of nature," as Dumas significantly expresses it, " is destroyed," and as a necessary consequence the harmony is disturbed, and sickness and death are the result to the disturbers. All the operations of nature tend to produce unity and harmony in their results ; and whenever man interferes with that order, it is at the expense of his health and well-being.

While preparing an article on cholera, as it appeared at Burlington, Iowa, in 1850, I was forcibly struck with what I could not but regard as the preventive influence of trees. In the houses on the

---

* Becqueral, *Des Climats.*
† Salvagnoli, *Rapporto sul Bonificamento delle Maremme Toscane.*
‡ *Il Politecnico, Milano,* 1863.
§ Parkes' *Practical Hygiene.*

west side of Main Street, north of Court, more deaths took place than in any other portion of the city; and that more occurred in proportion to the number of inmates in every other house, than in the one in front of which were trees; and what is still more convincing, the natural predisposition to cholera existed to a greater extent among the inmates of this house, than in any other. Another and more striking instance occurred in the two houses nearest the "Old Saw Mill." The house adjoining the mill was surrounded by trees and not one of the occupants suffered from cholera; while, in the other house, which was exposed and stood upon the bank of the Mississippi, three deaths took place; and what is more to the point is, that the family which escaped, were new-comers and suffering from nostalgia and the effects of a change of climate, which act as a predisposing and exciting cause of the disease; while those who lived in the other house, were old residents, and had been thoroughly acclimated. Dr. Buckler notices similar facts in his account of the cholera as it appeared in the Baltimore Alms-House, in 1849.

In the summer of 1852, the trees on the high bluff in the northern part of Burlington, were cut down. It was not until the months of August, September, and October, of the following year, that any apparent effect of this destruction of the trees took place, when nearly all who lived in that portion of the city suffered with fevers, and several of them died.

During the late war of the Rebellion, much of the sickness of the army of the Potomac in the summer, autumn, and winter of 1861, while encamped near Washington, was the result of the destruction of the trees for purposes of defence, as a military necessity, and for the use of the troops. The same was also noticed in Louisiana, where troops had been encamped for some time, and many trees were cut down. This was strikingly illustrated at Port Hudson, where, for purposes of defence, the rebels cut down nearly all the timber adjoining the outer fortification. It became necessary, in several places, to cut down more by our troops, and in a very short time the effect was quite marked in the increase of sickness, exclusive of casualties, in the regiments camped upon or near this ground.

TREES MODIFY CLIMATE.

We next propose to consider how far trees modify climate. Their shafts may be regarded as so many pipes for conveying heat from the earth to the air in winter, and from the air to the earth in the summer ; and this effect in modifying the range of temperature, as indicated by repeated experiments, is far from being insignificant. In summer, plants and trees, in addition to their conducting powers, render the atmosphere cooler by the great quantity of water that is exhaled from the leaves during foliation. Hales found that a sun-flower three and one-half feet high, with a surface of 5.616 square inches, exposed to the air, perspired at the rate of twenty to thirty ounces avoirdupois every twelve hours, or seventeen times more than a man.* A vine with twelve square feet of foliage exhales at the rate of five or six ounces a day ; and a seedling apple-tree, with eleven square feet of foliage, lost nine ounces a day.

An experiment, performed by Bishop Watson, will assist in giving an idea of the extraordinary amount of change effected by this function in plants. He placed an inverted glass vessel, of the capacity of twenty cubic inches, on grass which had been cut during a very intense heat of the sun, and after many weeks had passed without rain ; in two minutes it was filled with vapor which trickled down its sides. He collected these drops on a piece of muslin, which he carefully weighed ; and repeating the experiment for several days, between twelve and three o'clock, he estimated as the results of his inquiries, that an acre of grass transpires in twenty-four hours, not less than 6,400 quarts of water. This is probably an exaggerated statement, as the amount transpired during the period of the day in which the experiment was tried, is far greater than any other.†

When we consider the vast perspiring surface presented by a large tree in full leaf, it is evident that the watery vapor it exhales is immense. "The Washington Elm," at Cambridge, a tree of no extraordinary size, was some years ago estimated to produce a crop of seven millions of leaves, exposing a surface of 200,000 square feet, or about five acres of foliage. ‡

The refreshing coolness, then, of a grove on a hot summer day is not to be wondered at ; and how often have we, while enjoying it, inquired what was the cause, simply supposing it was the result of shade. This exhalation is dependent on the capacity of the air for moisture, at the time, and the presence of the sun, while frequently it is scarcely perceptible at night.

---

* *Vegetable Statics.*
† Carpenter's *Comparative Physiology.*
‡ Gray,—"*How Plants Grow.*"

4

In like manner, trees act as conductors of heat from the earth in winter, because the surrounding atmosphere is cooler than the earth in which they grow. It is true that the conducting power of wood is slow, which is much less transversely to the direction of its fibre, than with it,* which would prevent the interior of a large trunk from being rapidly affected by the change in the heat of the external air; and accordingly, it is found that the larger the trunk in which the observation is made, the greater the difference.† Trees possess a specific temperature of their own, independent of their conducting power,—an organic activity for generating heat, like that with which the warm-blooded animals are gifted, though by a different process, which has undoubtedly some influence in estimating the action of the forest upon atmospheric temperature. The range of trees, apart from moisture, is restricted by temperature, and they have the power of withstanding the ordinary changes which take place during the year; but there are cycles of cold when, in certain species, the internal heat is overcome, and, as a necessary consequence, the life of the tree is destroyed. This is also shown in the protection that is necessary to young trees that are cultivated, to prevent their being destroyed by the ordinary winter temperature, owing to their vitality being insufficient to resist the depressing effect of cold; and such is also the case with young forest trees, as they will not grow unless protected by other and larger trees. It will therefore be seen that the same law obtains in the vegetable as in the animal kingdom.

After the leaves fall in the autumn, the rootlets continue to collect sap, and there is no doubt that some motion of the sap takes place even in winter, although the tree may be said to be asleep, as there is in reality only a diminution in the activity of its vital processes, which is a characteristic of all living beings, some heat must be evolved, which is greatly increased when the sap begins to flow actively and the terminal buds begin to swell.‡ It will, therefore, be seen that trees are the source of heat, in addition to the fact that they act mechanically in checking the force and movement of the winds, and thus cause the atmosphere surrounding them to be milder and less subject to sudden changes of temperature. It is the uninterrupted sweep of the winds, rather than the intensity of the cold, which abstracts from the vital energy of the system. The trapper

---

* Dr. Tyndall, *Phil. Transact.*, 1853.
† ‡ Carpenter's *Comparative Physiology.*

in the Hudson's Bay region, amid the stillness of the forest, day after day, pursues his accustomed round with the thermometer many degrees below zero, with little or no inconvenience; and so, too, with the lumberman in the pineries of Maine and Wisconsin. The human system is constantly giving out a volume of heat, which is abstracted more readily by the movement of the air than by mere radiation into space. This deprivation of carbonaceous matter, and the chilling and exhausting effect incident thereto, is but too well known and appreciated by the prairie traveler in winter. The same effect is apparent in operating a locomotive during very cold or windy weather, as it is found much easier to keep up steam while the engine is passing through woods than over the wind-swept ground, although the thermometer may indicate the same temperature. As soon as the train emerges from the shelter of the trees, the steam-gauge falls, and a more liberal supply of fuel is necessary to bring it up again.*

"Observation shows," says Meguscher, "that the wood of a living tree maintains a temperature of from 54° to 56° Fah., when the temperature stands from 37° to 47° Fah. above zero, and that the internal warmth does not rise and fall in proportion to that of the atmosphere. So long as the latter is below 67° Fah., that of the tree is always highest, but if the temperature of the air rises to 67° Fah., that of the vegetable growth is the lowest. Since, then, trees maintain at all seasons a constant mean temperature of 54° Fah., it is easy to see why the air in contact with the forest must be warmer in winter, and cooler in summer, than in situations where it is deprived of that influence." †

While engaged in investigating the nature of ozone, during the winters of 1851 and 1852, at Burlington, Iowa, I found that there was a difference of temperature between the western or Iowa bank of the Mississippi, (the wind was from the west, and the river frozen at the time,) and the eastern or Illinois side, of 2°, and penetrating the heavy forest that covered the bottom at that time, I found the temperature rising, until I reached about midway between the river and the prairie, where I found the temperature 16° higher, and it began to lower again upon approaching the edge of the prairie, although the wind was from the west, and, arrived at the prairie, I found the thermometer 4° lower than in the middle of the timber.

---

* In applying to the most prominent Railroad Superintendents of this city, their statement is unanimous, that during winter a far greater amount of fuel is consumed by a locomotive running through a prairie region than through one that is densely wooded.

† *Memoria sui Boschi di Lombardina.*

During the last six weeks, I have had three daily observations made of the temperature at the western, the middle, and the eastern portions of Wright's Grove, in the northern part of Chicago. I find as a general rule that the difference between the three points depends upon the direction of the wind, and the sudden changes of temperature ; the middle point being less affected, and ranging from one to seven degrees higher than either of the others. Some days there was no change perceptible in the three points, depending upon temperature and the activity of the wind. The period over which the observations extend has been remarkably mild, and one in which no sudden or great changes have taken place.

In comparing these observations with others made near the Artesian Well in the western part of the City, I find that only upon one occasion in a month, was the temperature as low as at the Well, while it ranged from one to nine degrees higher. In the month of December the thermometer, at 119 Randolph St.,[*] indicated 10° below zero ; at the Artesian Well, 17 ;[†] at the Observatory, 14 ;[‡] and at Wright's Grove, 12 ; at the same time, the wind being from the south-west.

Trees and plants exercise a marked influence on the humidity of the air, causing its moisture to be more equally distributed. They also act as excitors or conductors of electricity,[§] and it is supposed in countries where hail storms are frequent and destructive, that they occur in proportion as the forests have been cleared.[‖] "Electrical action being diminished," says Meguscher, "and the rapid congelation of vapors by the abstraction of heat being impeded by the influence of the woods, it is rare that hail or water-spouts are produced within the precincts of a large forest when it is assailed by the tempest."[¶] May not the tornadoes which were so common throughout the North-west several years ago, be owing to our treeless prairies?

Trees may be regarded as climatological land-marks,[**] the destruction of which causes changes that may be restored by planting them. It is a well established fact that the climate of the older States

---

[*] J. G. Langguth.
[†] Wm. Giles.
[‡] Prof. Safford.
[§] Pouillet, "*Annales de Chimie.*"
[‖] *Le Alpi che cingono l'Italia.*
[¶] *Memoria sui Boschi, etc.*

[**] It has been a reproach to the aristocracy of England, that in a country where the agricultural capacity of the soil is so limited, and where population presses so closely on the heels of production, that vast tracts of land suitable for agriculture, should be appropriated to forests and the chase ; but those who make this charge, are little aware of the important part which these forests play in the climatology and health of the British Isles. They do not appreciate that forests make the atmosphere purer, and render the climate more equable, thus protecting them from sudden changes, and diminishing the amount of fuel and clothing necessary to their comfort.

has undergone a marked change in consequence of the destruction of the forests ;* viz., in the greater extremes of heat and cold, and in the perennial flow of the springs. This is manifest in its influence on man, in the altered character of the diseases, and also by the fact, that many manufacturing establishments which, a quarter of a century ago, had a water-power ample at all seasons to drive their machinery, are now compelled to resort, during the summer months, to the auxiliary aid of the steam-engine.

Trees are the highest type of vegetable life, and in many respects the greatest of living forms. What more imposing than one of the these monarchs of the forest, like the *Sequoia* of the Nevada Slope, towering up into the upper air for 400 feet, and with a shaft 30 feet or more in diameter at the base ! And then too, their antiquity. How many generations of men have disappeared, since first the germ of such a tree burst its seed-vessel ! Kit. North, than whom no one had a keener eye to the grandeur of the external world, thus speaks of these vegetable forms :

" Trees are indeed the glory, the beauty and delight of nature. The man who loves not trees—to look at them, to lie under them—to climb up them (once more a school boy)—would make no bones of murdering Mrs. Jeffs. In what one imaginable attribute, that it ought to possess, is a tree, pray, deficient? Light, shade, shelter, coolness, freshness, music, all the colors of the rain-bow, dew and dreams dropping through their umbrageous twilight, at eve or morn, dropping direct—soft, sweet, soothing and restorative from heaven. Without trees, how in the name of wonder could we have had houses, ships, bridges, easy chairs or coffins, or almost any single one of the necessaries of life. Without trees, one man might have been born with a silver spoon in his mouth, but not another with a wooden ladle.

" Tree, by itself, tree, · such tents the patriarchs loved.' Ipse nemus ' the brotherhood of trees '—the Grove, the Coppice, the Wood, the Forest—dearly and after a different fashion, do we love you all ! And love you all we shall, while our dim eyes can catch the glimmer, our dull ear the murmur of the leaves, or our imagination hear at midnight the far-off swing of old branches groaning in the tempest. Oh ! is it not merry, also sylvan England ? And, has not Scotland, too, her old pine forests, blackening up her highland

---

* It has been observed in Sweden, that the spring, in many districts where the forests have been cleared off, now comes on a fortnight later than in the last century.—Asbjörsen, *Om Skovene i Neye.*

mountains? Are not many of our rivered valleys not unadorned
with woods—her braes beautiful with their birkin shaws? And does
not stately ash, or sycamore, tower above the kirk-spire, in many a
quiet glen, overshadowing the humble house of God, the dial stone,
aged and green, and all the deep sunk, sinking, or upright array of
grave-stones, beneath which *

'The rude forefathers of the hamlet sleep.' "

LOCAL CONDITIONS.

We now come to consider the local conditions by which we are
surrounded, both terrestial and atmospheric, in connection with their
influence upon man, particularly in causing disease. In these are
included the topography, nature of soil, temperature, winds, rains,
and humidity of the atmosphere, all being more or less intimately
connected, as there is no doubt that the surface controls the
atmosphere, as much as the atmosphere controls the surface.

Chicago is situated in latitude 41° 52′, longitude 78° 35′, and is
591 feet above the level of the sea. The surface is nearly a flat level
and treeless plain, on the south-western shore of Lake Michigan.
The highest point above the level of the Lake for fifteen miles north,
is 38 feet,† and south-east for the same distance, 23 feet,‡ near the
Chicago University; from thence there is a gradual descent to the
Calumet, when the ground gradually rises. Directly south of the city
the surface is almost level, as the highest point in sixteen miles is
only 22 feet.§ The topography south-west is still more remarkable,
as for twenty miles, the highest point above the level of the lake is
at Summit, only 10 feet, where the waters of the St. Lawrence run
north-east. From the Summit there is a gradual descent, until the
ground is lower than the surface of the lake. At twenty miles
it is only 1 foot above the lake. ‖ Three miles directly west,
the surface is 17 feet; five miles, 20 feet; seven miles, 27
feet; at Austin, where no doubt was once the shore of the lake,
and continuing 2½ miles farther at Harlem, we find an elevation

---

* *"Noctes Ambrosianæ."*
† Milwaukee R. R.
‡ City Engineer.
§ Rock Island R. R.
‖ Alton & St. Louis R. R.

of 48 feet, the highest point in any direction within ten miles of Chicago. Continuing to the Des Plaines there is a descent, the bottom of the river being 26 feet; then there is a marked increase in the ascent, so that at fifteen miles the surface is 102, and at twenty miles 125 feet above the level of the lake.* North-west of the city, at four miles, we only find an elevation of 10 feet; at seven miles of 27 feet, where we again strike the original lake shore; at ten miles, 40 feet; at eleven miles, 65 feet; at twelve miles, 82 feet; from this point there is a gradual descent to Des Plaines River, where the elevation is 33 feet; thence the ascent is gradual and at twenty miles distant it is 96 feet.† It will be seen from the foregoing that the highest point within five miles of the mouth of Chicago River, in any direction, is only 23 feet, and for ten miles, 48 feet above the level of the lake; and that a large portion of this ground is low and swampy, with but little surface drainage, and an average elevation of about 12 feet. As a necessary consequence, as in all plains, great and sudden changes of moisture and temperature take place. The winds, meeting with no obstruction, have full sweep; in fact, the topography of the surroundings of the city tends to this result, favoring even the prevailing winds of this latitude. The only interruption in this open plain to the winds, may be said to be the narrow belt of timber on the Des Plaines, and with here and there an occasional patch of thinly covered wood-land, on the elevations which once were the shores of the lake. With this exception, the open plain may be said to continue for a great distance north-west, west, and south-west. It is true, timber is scattered north and south, but unfortunately not enough to materially influence the climate, in addition to the fact that the winds are rarely from either direction. In an area of 400 square miles surrounding Chicago, there are only about 20 square miles thinly covered with timber; ten of these are found on the north side of the city, and along the North Branch of Chicago River; five south and south-east; and ten on the ridges six miles west, and in the valley of Des Plaines River.

LAKE MICHIGAN.

Of all the local conditions that obtain at Chicago, none exercise a greater influence on the climate than Lake Michigan. It moderates the extreme cold of winter, and the oppressive heat of summer; increases the humidity of the atmosphere, and the

---

* Northwestern R. R.
† Galena R. R.

quantity of rain that falls, and causes local currents of air, thus
partially changing the prevailing winds of this latitude, producing
necessarily local changes of temperature.   These local undulations
are most marked in the spring, owing to the fact that the specific
heat of land is only one-quarter that of water, and it both absorbs
and gives it out more rapidly ; while water, on the other hand,
absorbs it more slowly, stores up a greater quantity, and parts with
it less readily, owing, no doubt to the difference in the conducting
and radiating properties of both.   It is mainly owing to this fact
that our springs are so cold, raw, and long continued ; that is, the
water is not as soon heated as the land, thus giving rise to local
changes of temperature, and of winds.   In the autumn the heat
of the water is less readily abstracted than that of the land, thus
causing the temperature in the immediate vicinity of the lake to be
milder than even at localities further south and west, as, during
last September, October, and November, the mean temperature
of Springfield, was nearly the same as at Chicago.*   This was no
doubt owing to the fact that the temperature of the lake was more
than ordinarily high in July and August; as, on July 20th, the thermometer indicated $72°$† at a depth of thirty feet, while the mean
temperature of the air, on the same day, was $83°$, and even
later the extraordinary warmth of the water that passed through
the Tunnel attracted attention, and it was supposed that the water
supplied to the city, did not come through the Tunnel, and that an
accident had occurred, and the supply was being pumped up from
near the shore.   The mean temperature of the lake is no doubt the
same as that of the land for the year, differing only in the absorbing
and parting power of heat; as is evidenced by the fact that the
freezing point only obtains a short distance from the shore.   It will
therefore be seen how, for eight months of the year, and sometimes
even nine, the lake exercises a wholesome influence upon the health,
counteracting, to some extent, the great and sudden changes incident
to our level and open topography, while during the remaining
months it is injurious to health, on account of the cold and chilling
effect it has, in addition to causing sudden changes.   Owing to its
large evaporating surface, it supplies a large amount of the oxygen
that is consumed here, thus purifying the atmosphere.

---

* *Agricultural Bureau Reports.*
† Langguth

GEOLOGY.

The geological structure of the region embracing Chicago and the surrounding country is exceedingly simple. The underlying rock is the Niagara limestone which has a general dip to N. N. E., and consequently sinks deeper as traced lake-ward. This rock is seen at the surface at several points in the city and vicinity. Upon this floor was originally deposited a mass of blue clay, not less than one hundred feet in thickness, but as traced toward the former rim of the lake it rapidly thins out. This rim is clearly defined in one or more terraces, which are traceable from the head of the lake far into Indiana, but to the west of the city 8½ miles distant, at Harlem, they constitute the divide between the waters of Lake Michigan and the Mississippi. While the lake has receded far below its former level, it has left behind a series of sand ridges, the intervals between which are occupied by ponds, which by reason of the sluggish flow of the water and their sheltered position, have proved favorable to the growth of peat-producing plants, from whose decay have resulted large accumulations of humus or vegetable matter. It is upon this ancient lake-bed that the city is founded. The original surface was diversified by sand banks, most abundant along the lake shore, extending occasionally to the depth of 16 feet, by partly filled lagoons, and a vegetable mould (which covers the greater portion of the city), resting sometimes on blue clay, and sometimes on beds of sand and gravel, and occasionally mixed, — the depth of these being governed by their proximity to the Chicago river and its branches. The whole region was originally low, flat and ill-drained. Some of the business blocks are built upon partly filled lagoons. In the soundings made by Mr. Chesbrough, City Engineer, preparatory to completing the Tunnel for the Water Works, it was found that the lake-bed was composed of blue clay with superficial sands above, which shifted in every heavy storm.

Such a soil must necessarily exercise a decided influence upon the health of those living upon it, depending of course whether their houses rest upon sand, clay, or humus. Sandy soils absorb and retain heat much longer, while the clays and humus are cold, and absorb heat slowly. Sand absorbs and retains little water; clays twenty times more; and humus, or surface soil, fifty times more than sand; and in this way, to some extent, the relative healthfulness of different portions of this city, and even of wards, can be accounted for.

5

WINDS—Their Influence on Health.

Winds are the result of changes of temperature and the pre-cipitation of moisture, acting as changes of density, and as the movements of bodies would act to produce currents and movements in a mass of water.* This is the strictly meteorological definition, but in a sanitary point of view, there are none of the atmospheric phenomena that exercise a greater influence for good or evil. The free movement of air in summer, in certain localities, is beneficial in dissipating noxious emanations, and purifying the atmosphere, while in the same locality, in the cold season, it abstracts heat, depending, of course, on its velocity and humidity, and thus acting injuriously upon life. The seeds of disease are frequently wafted by winds over unhealthy localities, and thus causing those who live quite remote from the exciting cause to suffer. Fevers and acute pulmo-nary and inflammatory diseases do not usually manifest themselves under the influence of the same wind, although fever and certain other diseases may occur in connection with any currents which waft the air from the neighboring surfaces, where the elaboration of the morbific cause is going on.

NORTH WIND.

The north wind is less frequent than any other. It generally exercises a beneficial influence, and in winter is the mildest, with the exception of the south-east and east, owing to the lake and the trees found north of the city. In summer it is cool and refreshing. This wind, like all others, is influenced by locality in its effects upon health, as in New Orleans, in summer, it always causes sickness.

NORTH-EAST WIND.

The north-east is the most common wind in spring and summer. In the months of March, April, and May, it is a cold, moist wind, and continues so until the temperature of the earth is higher than that of the lake, when it becomes cool and pleasant, remaining so until November, or until the temperature of the earth becomes lower than that of the lake. This wind increases pulmonary, rheumatic and inflammatory diseases in spring, and is the main reason why that season of the year is so long-continued and unpleasant; but during extreme heat and cold it is beneficial. The north-east wind blows malarial fever into portions of Rome. In Batavia this wind

---

* Blodgett's *Climatology.*

is highly unfavorable to health. On the west side of the town of Marenne, in France, are situated vast marshes, and when the wind blows from the north and north-east, fevers are rare ; but when the wind blows from the west, south-west, or south, so as to pass over these surfaces before reaching the town, fevers make their appearance. On the contrary, at Saint Agnant, situated opposite to Marenne, and on the other side of the marshes, the conditions are reversed, and during the prevalence of the east wind the town becomes sickly.

EAST WIND.

The east wind, with the exception of the north, is the least frequent, and is more common in spring than any other season of the year. In winter it is warm, and while from this direction there is a diminution in the number of cases of acute inflammatory diseases, and only a short time in spring is it disagreeable. The lake exercises a marked influence upon this wind, and that from the north-east. Edinburgh is supposed to be subject to fever through the agency of the east wind which wafts it from Holland, and the same wind wafts malaria from Essex to London.

SOUTH-EAST WIND.

Of all the winds, none is so depressing and enervating as the south-east. It is a warm, moist wind, oppressive to man and beast, in consequence of checking evaporation, thus raising the temperature of the body, and causing the lungs to exhale a larger amount of carbonic acid than usual,[*] and in this way exhausting the vital energies. In addition to the ordinary effect of a warm, moist wind, it is loaded in the summer and autumn with the noxious exhalations of the swampy region south-east of the city bordering on the lake and Calumet river. The topography of the country south and south-east of the city is such as to promote currents of air from this direction, and even to direct them toward the city, as they meet with but little obstruction, causing this wind to be more frequent than if such were not the case, it being here more of a local than general wind. When the weather has been intensely cold for a number of days, a change to this direction, will diminish mortality, but for at least nine months of the year it is the most fatal wind. In the summer and autumn, even when no epidemic tendency exists, a change to this direction generally terminates fatally to nearly all diseases, where the patient

---

[*],Lehmann.

has been hanging, as it were, "in the balance." It also increases all
infantile and bowel affections. The most marked change that I have
noticed, occurred on July 16th, 1868, when the wind blew from the
north-east, and the mortality was 21; on the 17th it changed to the
south-east, and 38 died; 18th, wind continuing from the same direction, 63 deaths (the highest mortality in a single day for two years,)
occurred, the mean temperature of the two days being nearly 86
degrees. On the 19th, the wind changed to the north-east, and
the mortality diminished to 35, with a mean temperature of 77.66
degrees. It was at this time that the greatest mortality occurred in
the 12th ward, in the extreme north-western ward of the city. This
fact clearly shows that its poisonous qualities, were added to the noxious emanations of the city, increasing in its intensity as it progressed
north-westward. This wind carries with it the plague to Constan-
tinople and various parts of Russia and Poland, in fact, to all the
countries of Europe bordering on the Mediterranean. It produces
an unfavorable influence on the health of London and Dutch Guiana.
At Burlington, Iowa, in July, 1850, the wind was in this direction
during the prevalence of the cholera as an epidemic, but upon its
changing to the north-west, the disease immediately abated, and the
cholera re-appeared a few days after, when the wind changed again
to this direction. Here the wind passed over the Mississippi bottom
on the Illinois side. In 1851 the cholera broke out at Oquawka,
Illinois, fifteen miles above Burlington, while the wind was from
the west. Here the low lands and swamps are on the Iowa side.
At this time there was no cholera at Burlington.

SOUTH WIND.

The south wind is more common than either the east or north. It
is most frequent in winter, and it is rarely that it is for a day from this
quarter, and then only when the wind is shifting from the south-west
to the south-east, or from the south-east to the south-west. The
ground directly south of the city is unfavorable to this current, as
the surface of the country rapidly rises beyond Blue Island, forming
depressions both east and west. In winter the south wind exercises
a beneficial influence in moderating the extreme cold of the westerly
winds, diminishing the mortality, and the same result is observable
in spring. In the summer it prevails only when great changes have
taken place, and its influence is quite marked, as between the damp
south-east, and the dry south-west. In autumn its effect on health is
not apparent.

SOUTH-WEST WIND.

The prevailing wind, not alone of Chicago, but of the greater portion of the valley of the Mississippi, is the south-west. In 1868, it was the hottest and coldest,* and, when great disturbances take place, the same has been observed to occur within the short period of a month. In the summer it is hot, dry and relaxing, causing at first free evaporation ; but if long continued, it produces harshness and dryness of the skin, and general malaise ; in winter it is dry, cold, and sharp. It partakes of the character of the country, and of the seasons ; the surface being a flat, level plain, with an altitude of only 10 feet above the level of the lake at the highest point, necessarily a large portion swampy, with nothing to impede its sweep, plainly showing how it may alternately be the hottest and coldest, even in so short a period as a month. It is the normal wind of the summer and autumn in this latitude, but owing to the local topography, and the great and sudden changes incident thereto, it alternates in frequency, between summer, autumn, and winter. This wind having a greater elaborating surface than any other, necessarily exercises a great influence upon health, in addition to its wafting the malarious exhalations of Mud Lake, and the region contiguous to the Illinois and Michigan canal, over every portion of our city, and next to the south-east is the most fatal ; and, owing to its being the most prevalent wind, causes the greatest mortality.†

* In 1867 a very able and interesting memorial was presented to the Michigan Legislature, in obedience to instructions received from the State Board of Agriculture by T. T. Lyon and Sanford Howard, Esqrs., on the change of climate caused by the destruction of the forest trees, and the consequent injurious effect upon crops and fruit trees, petitioning the Legislature to enact laws to prevent the unnecessary destruction of the forests, and to encourage the planting of trees, as a means of shelter and protection to crops and fruit trees. In this report they alluded to the change that had taken place in the older portion of the State, within the last thirty years, in the extremes of heat and cold ; the greater prevalence and force of the winds ; resulting in the destruction of peach trees, wheat, corn, and the winter killing of clover. The memorial says: " Last year the loss in all that part of the State lying south of the Michigan Central Railroad,'a region deprived of the ameliorating influence of Lake Michigan, or the south-west wind, and composing the richest agricultural portion of the State, was estimated at no less than three-fourths of the entire wheat crop ! From what enquiries your committee have been able to make, the loss on the wheat crop alone, of this State, for the last four years, is not less than $20,000,000. Your committee would be most happy to believe that this enormous loss springs from causes evanescent in their nature, and destined speedily to pass away, to return nevermore. But your committee are fearful that these vast losses "are but the beginning of sorrow," and that the improvidence which laid our open fields to that scourge of God, the south-west wind, by the wholesale destruction of our forests, is now only beginning to reap the fruit of that want of forethought, and that these losses can be avoided only by restoring, in part at least, the natural barriers against the wind."
Diagrams are given showing the influence of the winds on temperature and rain, for four years, at Lansing, clearly demonstrating that the conclusions of the committee were based upon facts. An examination of the topography of the lower and central portions of Michigan will show the cause of the frequency and influence of the south-west wind. The Legislature, with commendable judgment and foresight, passed a law encouraging the planting of trees and shrubs along the highways, also providing for their care and protection.
† The effect of this wind on the health of the city, particularly in summer and autumn, will be appreciated, when it is borne in mind that a large extent of the surface over which it passes before reaching the city, is covered by water in the spring, which is evaporated during the summer and autumn, leaving the large quantity of humus, or vegetable mould that covers it, exposed to the influence of the sun and air, in addition to liberating a large portion of the carbonic acid that is held by the soil. What makes it still worse, is the fact that but little of the soil for miles in this direction is cultivated.

WEST WIND.

The west wind is more common than any from the direct points of the compass, and is most frequent in winter, when it is generally the coldest and driest, owing to the fact that the ground is higher and drier than in any other direction. The greatest mortality, when this wind prevails in winter, is by acute inflammatory diseases, and occasionally in autumn and spring; but in summer a change to this quarter from the south is cooling to the atmosphere and invigorating, and its influence is marked in a great diminution in the number of deaths. Generally speaking, less mortality occurs than from any other direction, and it may be said to be the healthiest wind during the entire year.

NORTH-WEST WIND.

The north-west wind might with propriety be called Boreas, as it is a cold, fierce, and penetrating wind in winter; in spring cold, blear and bleak; and in summer cool and refreshing. The topography of the country north-west of the City tends to the formation of currents in this direction, at the same time there being no obstructions to their full sweep, their velocity is greater than from any other quarter. In fact the character of the country over which it passes is impressed upon it, as it is occasionally the coldest, but never the warmest. It is pretty equally divided in frequency between winter, spring, and autumn, and is least prevalent in summer. Its influence on health is most marked in winter, and particularly in spring when it causes great changes of temperature, resulting in pulmonary, rheumatic, neuralgiac, and inflammatory diseases, while in the summer it diminishes mortality, and exercises a wholesome influence upon health.

I do not wish to be understood as saying that winds alone are the cause of death, but that owing to local causes they increase mortality, which would not be the case if these conditions did not obtain. While I fully appreciate the important part they play in purifying the atmosphere, I do mean to say that in some seasons certain winds increase mortality, or, in other words, that there are times *here* when we have too much wind, as I have already shown that this may be the case in winds from any direction.

The following tables have been prepared with much care, the facts having been obtained from all sources at my command, and will corroborate what I have said with regard to the prevalence and influence of winds.

TABLE SHOWING DIRECTION OF WIND, HIGHEST, LOWEST, MEAN, AND RANGE OF THERMOMETER, WITH RAIN, SNOW, AND MORTALITY, BY MONTHS, FOR FIVE CONSECUTIVE YEARS.

1859. Population — 101,780.

	DIRECTION OF WIND.									TEMPERATURE.						
	N.	N.E.	E.	S.E.	S.	S.W.	W.	N.W.	No. of Observations.	H.T.	L.T.	M.T.	RANGE.	RAIN No.Days	SNOW.	MORTALITY.
January	1	8			9	26	13	5	62	44	-8	27.8	52	5	4	131
February	2	4	3	6	4	20	8	9	56	58	1	32.4	57	6	10	115
March	4	8	4	6	3	27	8	2	62	62	26	41.7	36	8	3	132
April	5	24		7		10	14		60	58	26	41.6	32	11		155
May	3	22	1	4	5	21	2	4	62	82	42	59	40	8	4	115
June	2	20	4	8	2	14	9	1	60	90	41	62.3	49	6		112
July	7	18	7	15	2	10	1	2	62	95	52	75.5	43	4		164
August	4	7	17	14		8		4	54	91	55	68.8	36	7		325
September	2	14	2	11	4	16	2	9	60	74	46	62.6	28	5		190
October	3	10		2	6	17	18	6	62	76	26	49.4	50	8	1	160
November	2	5	2	13	8	10	13	7	60	70	16	40.2	54	9	4	102
December	3	1		10	1	17	16	14	62	36	20	19.4	16	2	11	125
TOTAL	38	141	40	96	44	196	104	63	722					79	37	1,826

1860. Population — 109,260.

	N.	N.E.	E.	S.E.	S.	S.W.	W.	N.W.	No. of Observations.	H.T.	L.T.	M.T.	RANGE.	RAIN No.Days	SNOW.	MORTALITY.
January		1		4		27	21	9	62	50	-21	23.3	71	3	7	115
February	1	4		7	2	18	13	13	58	51	-5	30.6	59	6	7	128
March	14	3		7	4	16	15	3	62	71	23	42.6	48	4	3	180
April		26	5	9	3	6	6	5	60	76	32	47.8	44	8	2	131
May	1	15	10	6	2	10	7	11	62	87	34	61.5	53	7		102
June	8	14	6	8		8	6	8	60	88	50	65	38	7		155
July	2	21	2	8		14	3	2	52	89	58	73.2	31	14		288
August	2	21	7	10		13	2	7	62	86	58	72.2	28	7		308
September	4	8	3	16	3	12	4	9	59	84	43	62.7	41	10		174
October	5	12	8	5	4	9	2	17	62	77	35	53.7	42	7		149
November	2	6		10	4	11	13	13	62	55	4	37.3	51	12	3	170
December	4	1	5	6	3	10	16	17	62	46	8	25.5	38	3	11	158
TOTAL	43	132	46	96	27	157	108	114	723					88	33	2,056

1861. Population — 123,623.

	N.	N.E.	E.	S.E.	S.	S.W.	W.	N.W.	No. of Observations.	H.T.	L.T.	M.T.	RANGE.	RAIN No.Days	SNOW.	MORTALITY.
January		2	3	8	4	13	15	16	61	40	-3	24.4	43	2	7	173
February		1	6	7	2	21	8	11	56	60	-5	31.3	65	2	8	135
March	5	7	3	5	6	10	4	22	62	68	34	35.2	34	9	3	172
April	4	9	12	2	3	14	8	8	60	78	34	45	44	7		126
May	3	21	9	6	3	5	6	10	63	82	35	54.5	47	11		134
June	4	23	1	5	2	14	2	9	60	86	52	69.8	34	4		131
July	2	9	5	8		28	4	8	64	92	55	71	37	4		239
August	1	22		8	1	17	1	12	62	95	66	73.1	35	5		262
September	1	15	2	3	1	17	6	13	60	83	50	64.7	33	12		247
October	1	7	3	3	13	13	6	17	63	74	34	51.5	40	5		120
November	4	7	1	8	6	10	3	21	60	57	13	41.7	44	10	3	155
December	3	2	1	3	8	20	10	14	61	66	2	30.7	61	3	2	195
TOTAL	28	125	46	66	51	182	73	161	732					74	23	2,080

TABLE SHOWING DIRECTION OF WIND, HIGHEST, LOWEST, MEAN, AND RANGE OF THERMOMETER, WITH RAIN, SNOW, AND MORTALITY, BY MONTHS FOR FIVE CONSECUTIVE YEARS.—*Continued.*

1862. Population—138,186.

	N.	N. E.	E.	S. E.	S.	S. W.	W.	N. W.	No. of Observations.	H. T.	L. T.	M. T.	RANGE	RAIN No.Days	SNOW No.Days	MORTALITY.
January.....	....	12	2	8	3	11	7	19	62	38	-11	28.2	49	4	11	174
February ...	....	6	....	6	10	8	2	24	56	45	-8	24.3	53	...	6	197
March.......	10	21	4	3	4	6	4	10	62	50	16	36.8	34	....	2	199
April	8	23	8	2	7	7	2	3	60	72	32	46.9	47	14	....	187
May	3	19	12	8	4	11	3	2	62	82	40	55.9	42	13	....	168
June........	7	23	4	5	3	12	2	4	60	84	48	62.7	36	13	....	156
July	5	22	2	2	3	23	1	4	62	96	59	76.3	37	11	....	274
August.....	4	10	4	10	13	17	....	4	62	87	59	75.3	28	6	....	304
September..	5	7	6	7	21	9	3	2	60	83	46	65.2	37	12	....	271
October.....	4	6	1	8	5	24	1	12	61	89	30	55.2	52	3	2	246
November..	5	9	2	4	2	19	6	13	60	68	28	39.9	40	5	3	196
December ..	6	5	1	4	18	14	11	3	62	56	5	34.5	51	4	....	203
TOTAL....	57	163	46	67	93	161	42	100	729	....	....	....	....	85	24	2,575

1865. Population—178,492.

	N.	N. E.	E.	S. E.	S.	S. W.	W.	N. W.	No. of Observations.	H. T.	L. T.	M. T.	RANGE	RAIN No.Days	SNOW No.Days	MORTALITY.
January ...	....	6	....	1	2	37	4	12	62	50	-2	....	52	....	2	225
February ...	1	14	....	6	5	16	5	10	57	46	-16	....	30	1	8	256
March	4	9	6	5	....	25	4	9	62	70	3	....	67	3	3	279
April	....	19	2	6	....	18	4	11	60	76	18	....	58	15	2	230
May........	2	32	4	4	....	12	4	4	62	85	42	....	43	5	....	229
June	2	18	....	4	....	32	2	3	61	94	54	....	40	6	....	195
July	1	23	2	2	....	21	4	7	60	90	54	....	36	17	....	425
August.....	1	31	2	1	6	20	....	1	62	90	54	....	36	16	....	464
September..	6	1	4	4	12	27	4	2	60	90	52	....	38	10	....	316
October.....	7	13	4	4	14	8	7	5	62	78	30	....	48	8	1	360
November..	7	6	2	6	14	13	6	6	60	64	20	....	38	8	2	299
December ..	6	5	1	4	18	14	11	3	62	46	-10	....	56	2	5	333
TOTAL	37	177	27	47	71	243	55	73	730	....	....	....	....	91	23	3,661
TOT'L 5 Yns	203	738	205	372	286	939	382	511	....	....	....	....	....	....	....	....

The above table was partially compiled from a very able and interesting "Report on the Climate, Topography, and Epidemic Diseases of Illinois," by Dr. R. C. Hamill, of this city. I regret that the facts for 1863 and 1864 could not be obtained, this gap necessarily detracting from the value of the table. From even these imperfect data, it will be seen that owing to the constant climatic changes, great fluctuations of mortality occur; one year heavy and the next light, modified occasionally by epidemics. This fluctuation is the more striking when the constant increase in population is borne in mind, and they have been more marked since 1860 than before, particularly during the last five years.

	NO. OF OBSERVATIONS.								NO. OF DAYS.								MORTALITY.							
	N.	NE.	E.	SE.	S.	SW.	W.	NW.	N.	NE.	E.	SE.	S.	SW.	W.	NW.	N.	NE.	E.	SE.	S.	SW.	W.	NW.

1866

Month																								
January																								
February																								
March																								
April																								
May																								
June																								
July																								
August																								
September																								
October																								
November																								
December																								
TOTALS																								

Average Mortality per Day

1867 (January–December, TOTALS, Average Mortality per Day)

1868 (January–December, TOTALS, Average Mortality per Day)

TABLE SHOWING THE INFLUENCE OF THE CARDINAL WINDS ON MORTALITY AT CHICAGO.

1866. Population 200,418.

	Westerly Winds — No. of Days				Westerly Winds — Mortality				Easterly Winds — No. of Days				Easterly Winds — Mortality			
	S.W.	W.	N.W.	TOTAL	S.W.	W.	N.W.	TOTAL	N.E.	E.	S.E.	TOTAL	N.E.	E.	S.E.	TOTAL
Winter	28	23	9	60	247	214	88	549	6	3	12	21	45	26	146	217
Spring	16	15	21	52	110	119	205	434	19	7	7	33	153	80	61	294
Summer	27	12	13	52	483	195	293	971	19	1	10	30	427	17	304	748
Autumn	23	13	22	58	498	273	465	1236	16	3	14	33	604	67	381	1052
Total	94	63	65	222	1338	801	1051	3190	60	14	43	117	1229	190	892	2311

	Northerly Winds — No. of Days				Northerly Winds — Mortality				Southerly Winds — No. of Days				Southerly Winds — Mortality			
	N.	N.E.	N.W.	TOTAL	N.	N.E.	N.W.	TOTAL	S.	S.E.	S.W.	TOTAL	S.	S.E.	S.W.	TOTAL
Winter	1	6	9	16	10	45	88	143	8	12	28	48	88	146	247	481
Spring	4	19	21	44	38	153	205	396	3	7	16	26	27	61	110	198
Summer	4	19	13	36	77	427	293	797	6	10	27	43	168	304	483	955
Autumn	0	16	22	38	0	604	465	1069	0	14	23	37	0	381	498	879
Total	9	60	65	134	125	1229	1051	2405	17	43	94	154	283	892	1338	2513

1867. Population 225,326.

	Westerly Winds — No. of Days				Westerly Winds — Mortality				Easterly Winds — No. of Days				Easterly Winds — Mortality			
	S.W.	W.	N.W.	TOTAL	S.W.	W.	N.W.	TOTAL	N.E.	E.	S.E.	TOTAL	N.E.	E.	S.E.	TOTAL
Winter	17	20	17	54	166	191	181	538	15	3	11	29	162	27	152	341
Spring	17	10	20	47	154	88	167	409	27	5	12	44	233	40	121	394
Summer	19	5	12	36	354	22	186	562	22	4	32	58	348	38	601	987
Autumn	34	3	16	53	445	63	207	715	17	1	17	35	222	10	298	530
Total	87	38	65	190	1119	364	741	2224	81	13	72	166	965	115	1172	2253

	Northerly Winds — No. of Days				Northerly Winds — Mortality				Southerly Winds — No. of Days				Southerly Winds — Mortality			
	N.	N.E.	N.W.	TOTAL	N.	N.E.	N.W.	TOTAL	S.	S.E.	S.W.	TOTAL	S.	S.E.	S.W.	TOTAL
Winter	1	15	17	33	6	162	181	349	6	11	17	34	59	152	166	377
Spring	0	27	20	47	0	233	167	400	1	12	17	30	14	121	154	289
Summer	0	22	12	34	0	348	186	534	0	32	19	51	0	601	354	955
Autumn	1	17	16	34	19	222	207	448	0	17	34	51	0	298	445	743
Total	2	81	65	148	25	965	741	1731	7	72	87	166	73	1172	1119	2364

1868. Population 252,054.

	Westerly Winds — No. of Days				Westerly Winds — Mortality				Easterly Winds — No. of Days				Easterly Winds — Mortality			
	S.W.	W.	N.W.	TOTAL	S.W.	W.	N.W.	TOTAL	N.E.	E.	S.E.	TOTAL	N.E.	E.	S.E.	TOTAL
Winter	36	8	25	69	510	104	350	964	6	3	10	19	89	40	104	233
Spring	15	7	13	35	171	84	125	380	33	5	15	53	343	50	175	568
Summer	16	1	8	25	370	22	174	566	35	4	27	66	746	45	743	1534
Autumn	25	10	15	50	463	166	221	850	20	1	19	40	340	8	311	659
Total	92	26	61	179	1514	376	870	2760	94	13	71	178	1518	143	1333	2994

	Northerly Winds — No. of Days				Northerly Winds — Mortality				Southerly Winds — No. of Days				Southerly Winds — Mortality			
	N.	N.E.	N.W.	TOTAL	N.	N.E.	N.W.	TOTAL	S.	S.E.	S.W.	TOTAL	S.	S.E.	S.W.	TOTAL
Winter	2	6	25	33	23	89	350	462	1	10	36	47	13	104	510	627
Spring	4	33	13	50	38	343	125	506	0	15	15	30	0	175	171	346
Summer	1	35	8	44	7	746	174	927	0	27	16	43	0	743	370	1113
Autumn	1	20	15	36	10	340	221	571	0	19	25	44	0	311	463	774
Total	8	94	61	163	78	1518	870	2466	1	71	92	164	13	1333	1514	2860

DIRECTION OF THE WIND, TEMPERATURE, AND RAIN, BY SEASONS, AND THEIR INFLUENCE ON MORTALITY.

1866. POPULATION 200,418.*

	NO. OF OBSERVATIONS.								DAYS.								MORTALITY.									TEMPERATURE.				RAIN.
	N.	N.E.	E.	S.E.	S.	S.W.	W.	N.W.	N.	N.E.	E.	S.E.	S.	S.W.	W.	N.W.	N.	N.E.	E.	S.E.	S.	S.W.	W.	N.W.	TOTAL.	H.T.	L.T.	RANGE	M.T.	RAIN.
Winter	4	21	11	25	26	77	75	28	4	6	3	12	8	28	23	9	10	45	26	146	86	247	214	88	864	52	-18	70	26.8	5.200
Spring	5	53	24	25	18	46	48	54	5	19	7	7	3	16	15	21	38	153	80	61	27	110	119	205	793	85	11	74	49.00	8.652
Summer	24	53	3	18	27	77	49	31	21	19	1	10	6	27	12	13	77	422	17	304	168	483	193	293	1961	99	50	49	67.56	13.920
Autumn	6	48	6	36	4	74	43	53	6	16	3	14	....	23	13	22	....	604	67	381	....	498	273	465	2298	80	32	48	57.00	8.880

1867. POPULATION 225,326.†

	NO. OF OBSERVATIONS.								DAYS.								MORTALITY.									TEMPERATURE.				RAIN.
	N.	N.E.	E.	S.E.	S.	S.W.	W.	N.W.	N.	N.E.	E.	S.E.	S.	S.W.	W.	N.W.	N.	N.E.	E.	S.E.	S.	S.W.	W.	N.W.	TOTAL.	H.T.	L.T.	RANGE	M.T.	RAIN.
Winter	9	35	30	29	22	53	52	51	9	15	3	11	6	17	20	17	6	162	27	152	59	166	191	181	944	51	-18	69	27.6	5.257
Spring	8	67	23	33	6	30	32	42	....	27	7	12	1	17	10	20	....	233	40	121	14	154	83	167	812	71	-4	75	43.00	7.511
Summer	4	50	16	69	4	78	20	38	....	22	4	32	....	19	3	12	19	343	38	601	....	354	22	146	1549	94	46	48	72.7	5.707
Autumn	9	51	6	43	7	96	22	45	....	17	1	17	....	34	16	16	19	222	10	296	....	445	68	207	1269	51	39	12	54.4	3.448

1868. POPULATION 252,054.‡

	NO. OF OBSERVATIONS.								DAYS.								MORTALITY.									TEMPERATURE.				RAIN.
	N.	N.E.	E.	S.E.	S.	S.W.	W.	N.W.	N.	N.E.	E.	S.E.	S.	S.W.	W.	N.W.	N.	N.E.	E.	S.E.	S.	S.W.	W.	N.W.	TOTAL.	H.T.	L.T.	RANGE	M.T.	RAIN.
Winter	9	22	22	27	16	95	50	60	....	6	3	10	1	36	9	25	....	89	40	104	13	510	104	830	1233	56	-11	67	24.00	3.614
Spring	13	95	30	43	5	41	19	37	....	38	5	15	....	15	7	13	....	343	50	175	....	171	81	125	986	75	5	70	48.4	11.793
Summer	20	89	24	63	7	53	11	27	....	35	4	27	....	16	1	8	....	746	45	743	....	370	22	174	2107	100	50	50	73.9	10.558
Autumn	11	60	9	45	9	75	42	47	....	20	1	19	....	25	10	15	....	340	9	311	....	463	166	231	1519	84	26	58	52.4	11.370

*School Census. †Approximate. ‡School Census.

TABLE EXHIBITING THE RELATIVE MONTHLY TEMPERATURE OF THE WINDS, AT CHICAGO, WITH MEAN AND RANGE OF THE THERMOMETER, FOR THREE CONSECUTIVE YEARS.

January – March

Month	Winds	1866 Mean of Thermometer	1866 Range of Thermometer	1867 Mean of Thermometer	1867 Range of Thermometer	1868 Mean of Thermometer	1868 Range of Thermometer
JAN'Y	W. Coldest. / S.W. next. / N.E. " / N. " / S.E. " / S.W. War'st	26	56	32.5	57	20.4	45
FEB'Y	N.W. Cold't / S.W. next. / W. " / S. " / S.E. " / E. Warmest.	27	70	32.5	61	26.6	65
MARCH	W. Coldest. / N.E. next. / N.W. " / N. " / E. " / S.W. " / S. Warmest.	36	49	31	61	44	67

April – June

Month	Winds	1866 Mean of Thermometer	1866 Range of Thermometer	1867 Mean of Thermometer	1867 Range of Thermometer	1868 Mean of Thermometer	1868 Range of Thermometer
APR.	N.W. Cold't / W. next. / N.E. " / E. " / S.W. " / S.E. Warm't	53	45	46	38	45.90	54
MAY	N.E. Cold'st / N.W. next. / E. " / N. " / S.W. " / S.E. Warm't	58	45	51.4	27	55.38	32
JUNE	N.E. Cold'st / N.W. next. / W. " / S. " / S.E. " / S.W. Wrm't	70	49	72.4	38	67	38

TABLE EXHIBITING THE RELATIVE MONTHLY TEMPERATURE OF THE WINDS, AT CHICAGO, WITH MEAN AND RANGE OF THERMOMETER, FOR THREE CONSECUTIVE YEARS.—*Continued.*

Month	Year	Winds	Mean of Thermometer	Range of Thermometer
JULY.	1866	S.W. Hot'st, N.E. next, S.E. ", S. ", E. ", N.W. Cold't	70	37
	1867	S.W. Hot'st, S.E. next, N.E. ", W. ", E. ", N. E. Cold't	72.9	32
	1868	S.W. Hot'st, S.E. ", E. ", N. E., N. W. Cold't	81.09	30
AUG.	1866	S.W. Hot'st, W. next, S.E. ", N. ", N.W. ", N.E. Colds't	71	31
	1867	S.W. Hot'st, S.E. next, N. W. ", E. ", N. E. Cold't	72.5	32
	1868	S.E. Hot'st, S.W. next, S. ", W. ", N. W., N. E. Cold't	73.33	29
SEPT.	1866	S.W. Hot'st, S.E. ", N. E. ", W. ", N. W. Cold't	64	30
	1867	S.W. Hot'st, S.E. next, N.E. ", W. ", N.W. ", N. Coldest	66	41
	1868	S. E. Hot'st, S.W. next, N. ", E. ", N. W., N. W. Cold't	62.96	41
OCT.	1866	S.W. Hot'st, S.E. next, N. E. ", E. ", W. ", N.W. Cold't	60	41
	1867	S.W. Hot'st, S.E. next, N.E. ", N. ", W. ", W. Coldest	51.22	39
	1868	S.E. Hot'st, S.W. next, N.E. ", E. ", N. ", N.W. Cold't	52.67	37
NOV.	1866	W. Coldest, N.W. next, N. E. ", E. ", S. ", S.W. Wrm't	45	23
	1867	N.W. Cold'st, N.E. next, W. ", N.W. ", S. W. ", S. E. Wrm't	43.06	43
	1868	W. Coldest, N.W. next, N. E. ", S.W. ", S. E. Wrm't	41.70	39
DEC.	1866	W. Coldest, N.W. next, N.E. ", E. ", S. ", S.E. Warm't	38	43
	1867	W. Coldest, S.W. next, N.W. ", N. E. Wrm't	28.5	29
	1868	S.W. Cold'st, W. next, N.W. ", N.E. ", N. ", S. E. Wrm't	27.13	63

TABLE SHOWING TEMPERATURE, RAIN AND MORTALITY, BY MONTHS, FOR THREE YEARS.

	1866						1867						1868					
	Highest Temperature	Lowest Temperature	Range	Mean Temperature	Rain	Mortality	Highest Temperature	Lowest Temperature	Range	Mean Temperature	Rain	Mortality	Highest Temperature	Lowest Temperature	Range	Mean Temperature	Rain	Mortality
January	46	-10	56	26	.950	293	39	-18	57	22.5	1.926	299	41	-4	45	20.4	1.294	441
February	52	-18	70	27	1.050	260	51	-10	61	32.5	2.225	235	56	-9	65	27.8	.925	425
March	60	11	49	36	1.912	254	57	-4	61	31.3	1.594	280	72	+5	67	43.8	5.215	381
April	81	39	45	53	3.500	278	71	33	38	46.3	1.698	278	73	19	54	45.9	2.800	307
May	85	40	45	58	3.210	275	65	33	27	51.4	4.219	241	75	43	32	55.3	3.748	331
June	99	50	49	70	2.500	319	84	46	38	72.4	1.863	283	98	50	36	66.3	3.107	305
July	97	60	37	70	3.580	705	91	57	32	72.9	1.515	597	100	70	30	81.4	3.566	897
August	91	60	31	71	7.940	950	89	57	32	72.8	3.329	697	89	60	29	73.3	3.583	945
September	90	50	30	64	6.530	739	92	51	41	66	0.403	507	84	43	41	63.2	7.080	741
October	78	37	41	60	0.650	1170	81	42	39	54.2	1.217	426	74	37	37	52.9	1.690	448
November	65	32	23	45	1.500	383	69	26	43	43	1.768	370	59	26	33	41.9	2.600	401
December	50	7	43	38	3.200	309	39	10	29	28.5	1.106	409	52	-11	63	25.3	1.405	375
Amount of Rain during each year					36.652						21.863						37.335	
Rain for last six months of each year					23.500						8.398						20.226	
Mortality for last six months of each year						4,255						3,008						3,806
" for each year						5,935						4,644						5,956
Range of Thermometer for each year					117 F						112 F						111 F	
Mean " " " "					51.5"						49.5"						49.8"	
" " Barometer					29.38						29.26						29.21	

In the table on page 61, is shown the frequency of the wind from the different points of the compass, the number of days in which the winds prevailed, and the mortality that occurred on the days that the winds blew from the respective directions. It must necessarily be approximate, as the effect of the daily changes is not always manifest, and the fact, that frequently when the observations were made (three per day), the wind was from different directions, necessitating the study of each day separately and connectedly; representing in figures, as near as possible, the effect of the different winds on mortality. While there may be mistakes in single days, I am satisfied that in the main they are correct.

The following figures represent the average daily mortality for the last three years, when the wind prevailed from the different directions :

N.	N. E.	E.	S. E.	S.	S. W.	W.	N. W.
11.96	16.18	11,13	18.59	13.35	13.35	12.25	13.94

It will be noticed that the daily mortality for 1866, while the wind was from the north-east, was nearly as great as when it blew from the south-east. This result was caused by the cholera, which became epidemic in October. For four days, that is, from the 5th to the 9th, the wind was from the south-west, and dry, with a mean temperature of 65°. In the afternoon of the 9th, the wind changed to the north-west, reducing the temperature to 59°, the mortality increasing from 37 on the 6th, to 67 on the 9th. On the 10th, the wind changed to the north-east, with an increase of temperature of 3°, and the mortality reached 98 ; on the 11th, the temperature was 4° lower, and the deaths reached 71 ; on the 12th, the temperature rose 1°, and there were 82 deaths ; on the 13th, the temperature rose 3° higher, and there were 73 deaths ; on the 14th, the wind changed to the south-east in the morning, but veered again to north-east, when there were 61 deaths ; the same occurred on the 15th, with a lowered temperature of 4°, and 68 deaths ; on the 16th, the wind changed to the south-east, and there were 53 deaths ; and on the 17th, the wind changed to the south-west, and there were 43 deaths ; and from this time the number gradually diminished. It will be seen that, for four days in succession, the south-west wind prevailed ; and for four days the north-east ; and for two more, its influence was felt, with a higher temperature than has since been observed for the same length of time. On the 10th, 11th, and 12th, the motion of the air was barely perceptible, and was saturated with moisture, to such an extent as to partially obscure the sun, hanging over the city like a pall.

The high temperature and dry south-west wind had already paved the way for this great mortality ; and when to this was added the moist warm north-east wind, all the atmospheric conditions were prepared, and it only needed the presence of cholera to make it epidemic. Secretion of the skin was checked, the lungs were called upon to throw off an unusual amount of carbonic acid, thus reducing the vital powers, and the bowels were necessarily required to excrete more, and with what effect is but too well-known. This stillness of the atmosphere continued for three days, when, on the 14th, more activity was perceptible, with an abatement of the epidemic. The ratio would still be more marked, had a record been kept of all that died. That portion of the table referring to 1867, may be regarded as nearer the normal condition than that of either '66 or '68. The general health was remarkably good, but in 1868, there was a great increase of mortality, without any epidemic tendency, and the causes of which will be alluded to hereafter.

The table on page 62, shows the influence of Lake Michigan and of the cardinal winds upon life. It will be seen that more deaths occurred in 1866, when the westerly winds prevailed, and in the autumn, than at any other season ; also, in winter and spring, and that the greatest mortality occurred in summer by the southerly winds, and the least when easterly winds prevailed. In 1867, the mortality was more equally distributed between westerly and easterly winds, and the greatest number of deaths occurred during the prevalence of westerly winds, and in summer ; and that the least mortality took place in the spring, the season of the year when the causes of death are less rife than any other, unless more than ordinary conditions obtain. In 1868, the greatest mortality occurred during the prevalence of easterly winds, and in summer. This year, also, differs from the other years by the unusually great mortality that occurred in winter.

By reference to the table on page 63, will be seen the influence of temperature and rain on mortality, by seasons. During the winter of 1866, it was cold, and great mortality occurred during the westerly winds, not much rain falling ; in spring, it was warm, and the mortality was greater than usual, particularly when the north-west wind prevailed ; the summer was cold, and a large quantity of rain fell, and deaths took place proportionably ; and in autumn it was unusually warm, a large amount of rain also falling ; cholera prevailed, and the greatest mortality took place when the wind was from the north-east. From the 1st to the 21st day of October, the mean temperature was 63°. The winter of 1867 was milder than that of 1866, and, although there was a great increase in population, So more deaths occurred ; the spring was colder, and the mortality still less ; the summer was warmer than 1866, and the decrease in the number of deaths was still more marked ; the autumn was colder, and the mortality was not much over one-half as great. It will be observed that in this year (1867,) the mortality was more equally distributed between the westerly and easterly winds, and that the difference between the number that died while northerly and southerly winds prevailed, was nearer the normal number, and that the deaths were more equally distributed among the seasons than during either of the other years.

In 1868 the extreme cold of winter, with the extreme heat of spring and summer, and cold of autumn, with the unusual amount of rain that fell, greatly increased the mortality, although no epidemic prevailed. In the winter the mortality was unusually heavy, particularly during the prevalence of the north-west and south-west winds.

The tables on pages 64 and 65, illustrate the frequent changes of temperature in the direction of the wind, and in them may be found a record of the great climatic changes that have taken place here within the last three years.

A careful examination of the table on page 66, will show the influence of temperature and rain upon health. In that for 1866, will be noticed the mildness of January, the cold of February, the warmth of March, April, and May, the coldness of June, and extraordinary range of temperature, the warmth of July, and coldness of August, and, still more marked, that of September, with the extraordinary warmth of October, November, and December ; also, the great amount of rain that fell in the last half of this year, and all conditions conducing to and explaining the great fatality incident to that season of the year. In 1867 the temperature during the entire year was seasonable,—cold in winter, milder in spring, warm in summer, and pleasant in autumn, without any great extreme. About the usual amount of rain fell in the first half of the year, but in July, August, and September, an unusually small quantity fell. This season of dryness, in a sanitary point of view, was beneficial, owing to the want of drainage in a large portion of our city, in diminishing mortality. The influence of this equability of temper-

7

ature, and the small amount of rain that fell, is marked in the great diminution of deaths in all the months but January and December, as compared with 1866, although a great increase in population had taken place.

A striking contrast is, however, found in 1868, when the extremes of heat and cold were very marked, with the fall of an unusually large amount of rain. January and February were very cold, March warm, April cold, May warm, and June cold, July and August intensely hot; and from this time, the temperature gradually lowered, until the early part of December when it became intensely cold. The increase of mortality this year, compared with 1867, is great, although no epidemic prevailed, clearly demonstrating the influence of temperature and moisture upon health.

TEMPERATURE.

The frequent and sudden changes of temperature, at Chicago, are caused more by the winds than any other cause, owing to the open treeless plain upon which it is located, assisted by the evaporation from Lake Michigan. In the northern hemisphere the coldest month is January. In some parts of Canada, at Mackinac and Detroit, it is February; at Fort Snelling and St. Louis, in January. Here the mean temperature is coldest in January, rarely in February; in thirteen years the temperature was lowest for five years, in January; five, in February; and three, in December. The hottest month in most places is July; in a few, August; and at sea, it is always August. Here it is generally July, but sometimes it is August; and the highest temperature for thirteen years, was in June, four; July, six; and August, three times. The undulations of temperature are greatest in the interior of continents, remote from large bodies of water. Here, as well as at Toledo, Detroit, Mackinac and Milwaukee, the range is not as great as in the country south and west.

From observations made in the outskirts of the city, north, south and west, during the past year, I am satisfied that the range of temperature has increased at least two degrees, since the observations were made at Fort Dearborn, from 1832 to 1836, and that this increase in range is not as great north of the city, as south and west. The range north, for 1868, was 117°; south, 120°; west, 121°; while at 119 Randolph street, it was only 111°. The mean annual temperature has also increased about two degrees, although the observations made at 119 Randolph street, for the last three years, indicated a mean temperature of 50.2°. The extremes of heat and cold are more marked in the outskirts, than in the city, where, no doubt, the buildings have some influence in moderating the temperature ; as, by comparison, I find that in May, June, July, and August, it was colder in the heart of the city, but the remainder of the year it is colder on the outskirts. The only way in which this change of climate can be accounted for is, that since 1836, at least two-thirds of the timber that covered the country on which Chicago now stands, and its vicinity, has been destroyed, and that the region directly north of the city approximates nearer to the conditions that obtained, when the observations were made at Fort Dearborn, and that less timber has been destroyed there than in any other direction.* The following table, compiled mainly from the Army Medical Reports, for 1860, will give some idea of the relative temperature of the different localities, as compared with Chicago. Many of the observations extend over a long period, and were made before the settlement of the country had any influence upon the climate of the locality.

Annual Mean and Range of Thermometer.			Mean of Thermometer by Seasons.				
	MEAN.	RANGE.	SPRING.	SUMMER	AUTUMN	WINTER	
St. Louis,....................	54.56	125	54.15	76.36	55.44	32.27	12 Yrs.
Detroit......................	47.21	107	45.75	67.60	48.67	26.84	13 "
Mackinac....................	40.89	117	36.73	61.95	44.85	20.04	24 "
Sault St. Marie.............	40.40	131	37.53	62.21	43.54	18.32	31 ; "
Fort Howard................	44.49	138	43.52	68.51	46.01	19.91	21 "
Prairie du Chien.............	47.68	132	48.66	72.28	48.53	21.25	19 "
Rock Island................	50.23	130	50.52	74.12	51.42	21.88	11½"
Fort Ripley.................	39.30	147	39.33	64.94	42.91	10.01	6 "
Fort Snelling...............	44.52	140	45.54	70.61	45.89	16.05	35 "
Council Bluffs..............	49.28	129	49.28	74.76	51.36	21.73	7 "
Fort Laramie...............	49.91	133	46.84	71.94	50.32	30.54	6 "
Toledo*.....................	50.05	108	48.17	70.86	51.39	28.91	7 "
Milwaukee †................	46.07	111 ¶	43.68	67.44	48.81	20.47	22 "
Chicago.....................	46.75	116	44.90	67.33	48.84	25.90	1832–1836
Chicago‡................	50.26	113	46.80	71.38	54.60	26.13	1866–67–68
Near Chicago ǁ.............	47.77	120	47.00	75.00	48.69	20.40	1868
Chicago.....................	49.08	111	48.30	73.66	52.66	24.30	"
Lansing §....................	46.28	107	43.77	68.98	48.46	23.87	1866–67.

* Dr. Trembly.   † I. A. Lapham.   ‡ Langguth.   ǁ Brooks.   § Kedzie.
¶ Range for three years.

* Horticulturists and florists inform me that there is less danger from frost, and that generally speaking, the products of the garden thrive better north of the city than in any other direction.

RAIN.

With the change of temperature, I am of the opinion that less rain falls, and that there are greater extremes of wet and drought, than when the country was first settled, although the observations do not extend over a period sufficiently long to determine the fact. The following table will show the quantity of rain that fell at the several points for three consecutive years:

	1866.	1867.	1868.
Milwaukee....	33.96	24.62	29.37*
Toledo,............................	40.68	. ...	41.51†
Lansing,...............................	39.51	24.57	.....‡
Chicago,...............................	36.05	21.86	37.33

* Lapham.   † Trembly.   ‡ Kedzie.

It will be observed that the greatest extremes occurred at Chicago. The mean rain-fall at Milwaukee for 25 years is 30.20 inches; at Toledo, for six years, is 38.94; at Lansing, for four years, 30.56; and at Chicago, for the last three years, is 31.94 inches. The following table will show the quantity of rain that fell, when the winds prevailed from the different directions:

1867.

	N. E.	S. E.	N.	N. W.	S. W.	W.	E.
July, ...	.400	.115	....	.486	.505	....	...
August,....................	....	1.700	....	.775	.180	....	....
September,................	.844	.411	.028	....	....	....	....
October,..................	.112	....	....	.510	.486	....	....
November, ...	.015	....	....	.879	.852	...	....
December,................	.195	.341	. ..	.089	.271	.182	....
TOTAL, ...	1.575	2.627	.028	2.739	2.294	.182	....

1868.

	N. E.	S. E.	N.	N. W.	S. W.	W.	E.
January, ...	.115	....	....	.118	.549	....	.283
February,...................	.215	. ..	....	.550	....	....	....
March, ...	2.165	.390	....	.030	2.660	....	....
April,......................	1.275	.210	....	.420	1.095	....	....
May, ...	1.515	.045	.019	1.585	.210	.008	.285
June,.......................	1.216	.878	....	.011	.310	....	.680
July, ...	.388	.975	....	.485	1.120	....	....
August,..	.168	.350	....	.750	.545	....	1.740
September,................	2.780	....	....	1.980	2.250	.070	....
October,..................	.130	.510	.290	.750	....	....	.080
November,................	1.190	.600	....	.150	.210	.435	....
December, ...	.385	.080	....	1.830	.025	.085	....
TOTAL,..................	11.542	4.038	.239	8.659	8.974	.598	3.068

INFLUENCE OF CLIMATE ON THE MOST COMMON DISEASES.

The following tables* show the comparative mortality of certain diseases for the last three years; and, although the registration of deaths and the nomenclature of the diseases were very imperfect until 1867, when the present system of registration was inaugurated by the Board of Health, still they are sufficiently accurate to give a very good idea of the relative mortality, as influenced by climate for the different years. This will be better appreciated when I state, that in 1866, 475 deaths were reported from unknown causes, and as near as I am able to ascertain, about 500 deaths occurred of which no record has been kept. In 1867, 134 deaths were reported from unknown causes, and nearly all in the first six months, and about 100 deaths occurred of which no record has been kept. In 1868, only 28 are reported from unknown causes, and about 24 in which no record could be obtained. In judging of the comparative mortality, the increase in population must be taken into consideration.

THROAT AND LUNG DISEASES.

1866.

	January.	February.	March.	April.	May.	June.	July.	August.	September.	October.	November.	December.	TOTAL.
Bronchitis.....................	2	....	1	1	1	1	....	1	....	1	....	1	9
Croup.........................	20	18	12	16	9	9	15	9	6	8	11	7	149
Diphtheria...................	31	11	14	5	6	4	6	9	9	12	12	15	131
Laryngitis...................													...
Pleurisy...................	1	....	....	....	....	1	....	....	....	2	1	2	7
Pneumonia............... ..	19	22	27	25	14	8	14	15	9	3	13	13	182
Lungs, Congestion of...........	....	...	....	4	3	3	4	3	1	1	4	2	25
Consumption.............. ..	25	18	34	38	39	22	28	39	31	46	43	43	406
TOTAL..............	107	69	88	89	72	48	67	76	56	73	84	83	912

1867.

	January.	February.	March.	April.	May.	June.	July.	August.	September.	October.	November.	December.	TOTAL.
Bronchitis....	....	1	1	1	....	....	3	2	1	2	8	4	23
Croup.........	11	8	8	10	3	2	....	....	1	11	18	24	96
Diphtheria...................	8	6	5	6	7	1	3	4	5	10	9	11	77
Laryngitis...................	....	....	...	....	....	....	1	1	1	1	3	3	10
Pleurisy......................	....	....	...	....	....	3	....	....	....	....	....	....	3
Pneumonia.........	11	20	13	22	23	3	10	4	8	11	16	32	173
Lungs, Congestion of.........	2	7	1	2	3	2	4	2	1	1	1	4	30
Consumption...................	42	41	40	31	34	35	34	23	25	25	34	37	404
TOTAL...................	74	86	68	74	70	46	55	36	42	61	89	115	816

* Valuable assistance has been rendered, in the preparation of all the tables, by J. W. RUSSELL, Secretary, and H. P. WRIGHT, Clerk of the Board of Health; and I am indebted to Mr. J. G. LANGGUTH for all meteorological observations, not otherwise credited, taken at 117 Randolph Street.

THROAT AND LUNG DISEASES.—*Continued.*
1868.

	Jan.	Feb.	Mar.	April	May.	June.	July.	Aug.	Sept.	Oct.	Nov.	Dec.	Tor'L
Bronchitis...	11	12	9	3	8	3	....	3	3	8	6	9	75
Croup......................	8	12	11	6	6	8	3	6	11	18	10	18	112
Diphtheria....................	21	6	4	6	4	1	2	2	13	9	10	9	87
Laryngitis....................	5	1	2	3	2	2	....	2	2	....	2	....	21
Pleurisy.....................	2	3	2	....	....	1	1	....	1	2	....	....	12
Pneumonia...................	49	58	28	22	19	27	24	1	14	18	22	42	324
Lungs, Congestion of.........	9	5	3	3	3	1	3	3	5	4	4	4	47
Consumption...............	38	41	42	30	37	23	34	42	39	36	34	22	418
TOTAL................	143	138	101	73	79	66	67	59	88	95	88	99	1096

In the above table it will be seen that Bronchitis was more prevalent in 1867 than in 1866, and that there was a large mortality in 1868. This difference is owing to imperfect registration. Croup, a more common disease, was more frequent in 1866 than in 1867, and again, in 1868. Diphtheria was very prevalent in 1866, the mortality much less in 1867, and greater in 1868. Of Laryngitis, no deaths were reported in 1866, 10 in the last six months of 1867, and 23 in 1868. In Pleurisy, there was not much difference. The cases of Pneumonia for 1866, I am satisfied are too low, and that not all the deaths were reported, as there are only three less than in 1867, when the temperature was more equable and the extremes were not so marked as in 1866, or in 1868. The mortality by this disease in 1868 was very great in the months of January, February, March, and December, when the weather was extremely cold. A diminution occurred in April and May, when the weather was mild, with an increase in June, when it was again comparatively lower. It was also in January and February that most died of Small Pox, owing to its being complicated with Pneumonia, which is a common occurrence in the latter stages of the disease. In Congestion of the Lungs, the same discrepencies occur,—as, for the first three months, more deaths must have taken place in 1866 than in 1867, owing to the changes of temperature, as corroborated by the observations of 1868. Consumption, the most common and fatal of all diseases, is probably more correctly reported than any other. It being a hereditary and protracted disease, the effect of the changes of temperature is not as marked as in the acute pulmonary diseases, other causes tending to its fatal termination, such as occupation, confinement to a vitiated atmosphere, and depressing mental influences. It will be observed that more deaths occurred in the latter part of 1866, than the first half of 1867, than at any other time during the period under consideration. This would seem to indicate that the depressing effect incident to the visitation of Cholera in 1866, had some influence in increasing the mortality of this disease.

ABDOMINAL DISEASES.
1866.

	January.	February.	March.	April.	May.	June.	July.	August.	September.	October.	November.	December.	TOTAL.
Cholera	....	....	....	....	....	....	....	139	166	673	12	....	990
Cholera Morbus	....	....	....	....	....	....	10	15	36	15	4	....	80
Diarrhœa	1	5	3	3	2	3	21	38	21	21	5	5	128
Dysentery	2	1	....	3	3	6	29	29	13	10	2	....	98
Inflammation of Bowels	5	2	5	8	7	7	11	15	14	8	4	9	95
Gastritis	1	....	....	....	....	....	....	....	1	....	....	....	2
Hepatitis	1	....	1	....	....	....	....	....	....	4	1	1	8
Peritonitis	....	....	....	....	....	....	....	....	....	....	....	....	....
TOTAL	10	8	9	14	12	16	71	236	251	731	28	15	1101

1867.

	January.	February.	March.	April.	May.	June.	July.	August.	September.	October.	November.	December.	TOTAL.
Cholera	....	....	....	....	....	....	5	2	2	1	1	...	11
Cholera Morbus	....	....	....	....	1	....	1	....	1	....	....	....	3
Diarrhœa	4	1	5	2	7	2	3	45	47	12	4	5	137
Dysentery	....	1	....	....	2	1	11	24	20	13	5	2	79
Inflammation of Bowels	6	8	3	2	1	5	14	13	9	13	1	2	77
Gastritis	....	....	....	....	....	....	3	3	4	1	....	1	12
Hepatitis	2	2	....	1	....	....	....	....	1	1	1	1	9
Peritonitis	...	....	...	....	....	....	4	1	2	4	4	1	16
TOTAL	12	12	8	5	11	8	41	88	86	45	16	12	344

1868.

	January.	February.	March.	April.	May.	June.	July.	August.	September.	October.	November.	December.	TOTAL.
Cholera	....	....	....	...	....	....	....	....	....	....	....	....	....
Cholera Morbus	....	....	....	....	....	7	7	12	3	....	1	1	31
Diarrhœa	3	1	4	3	7	14	45	77	65	17	12	4	252
Dysentery	2	4	2	1	2	3	20	52	41	16	8	2	153
Inflammation of Bowels	8	3	6	2	5	2	15	14	13	7	4	1	80
Gastritis	4	1	4	....	4	1	3	5	2	1	....	2	27
Hepatitis	1	1	2	....	....	1	1	1	4	....	...	3	14
Peritonitis	2	3	2	....	....	1	1	....	1	2	...	....	12
TOTAL	20	13	20	6	18	29	92	161	129	43	25	13	569

This table shows that nearly all the deaths by Cholera occurred in 1866, a few in 1867, and none at all in 1868. In 1866, it will be remembered that all the climatic influences were favorable to the spread of diseases of this character, in addition to the fact that there was a decided epidemic tendency. In the last half of this year an extraordinary amount of rain fell, and the mortality by this disease was greatest in the low and undrained parts of the city, fully sustaining Pettenkofer's theory with regard to the influence of the "ground water" in this disease. In July and August, 1867, there was a marked tendency to Cholera, but less rain fell than in 1866, and every case was promptly taken care of, so that in not a single instance did a second case occur in the same house, even in those of patients who came from other cities and died. In 1868 there were no cases, and there was no epidemic tendency. It will be seen that cases of Cholera Morbus occur more frequently when great climatic changes occur. The same is the case with Diarrhœa, Dysentery, and Inflammation of the bowels. The difference in the number of cases of Gastritis, Hepatitis, and Peritonitis is simply of registration, for in the first period the registration in 1866, as compared with 1868, was imperfectly performed and the diagnosis was not accurately determined.

FEVERS.

1866.

	January.	February.	March.	April.	May.	June.	July.	August.	September.	October.	November.	December.	TOTAL.
Intermittent Fever............	1	1	1	....	....	....	....	....	....	....	....	....	3
Remittent Fever................	....	....	....	1	....	4	1	10	16	17	8	4	61
Congestive Fever............	....	....	....	1	2	3	....	....	....	....	....	....	6
Typhoid Fever	27	14	13	13	12	13	21	18	39	51	22	6	249
TOTAL.........	28	15	14	15	11	20	22	28	55	68	30	10	319

1867.

	January.	February.	March.	April.	May.	June.	July.	August.	September.	October.	November.	December.	TOTAL.
Intermittent Fever............	....	....	....	....	....	....	1	....	1	....	....	....	2
Remittent Fever................	3	2	3	....	....	....	....	....	1	1	...	....	10
Congestive Fever............	1	3	6	....	3	1	....	3	4	1	1	1	24
Typhoid Fever................	11	10	6	20	9	19	11	18	22	27	30	15	198
TOTAL...	15	15	15	20	12	20	12	21	28	29	31	16	234

1868.

	January.	February.	March.	April.	May.	June.	July.	August.	September.	October.	November.	December.	TOTAL.
Intermittent Fever............	1	....	1	....	....	....	....	3	1	1	....	....	7
Remittent Fever................	1	....	1	1	....	....	....	1	....	1	2	....	7
Congestive Fever...	...	1	....	1	....	....	3	2	. .	2	3	....	12
Typhoid Fever..	14	7	13	8	6	9	10	29	33	37	21	20	207
TOTAL..................	16	8	15	10	6	9	13	35	34	41	26	20	233

This table reveals the fact that the ordinary fevers are not very fatal here, and that few die of Intermittent Fever, the number being greatest in 1868. Remittent Fever killed more in 1866 than in either of the other years. Congestive Fever was most fatal in 1867 ; and I have no doubt that such was also the case, in 1867, with regard to Typhoid Fever, as a great many more cases occurred here during that year, owing to the dryness of the summer and autumn. I am satisfied that in 1866, a great many cases of cholera were reported as dying of Remittent and Typhoid Fevers, because they occasionally assumed a typhoid or low character and did not die for several days after the attack. Of the number reported, at least 70 are of this character, and it will be observed that the number of both diseases is much greater in the last half of the year than the first, and that there was suddenly a great falling off in Typhoid Fever for December, which is not the case in the other years for that month. My personal experience confirms this position, and when the remarkably small quantity of rain that fell during the year 1867, and particularly in summer and autumn, and the prevalence of Typhoid Fever are taken into consideration, although the mortality was not so very great, I am inclined to believe that the position assumed by Buhl* is correct, that Typhoid Fever increases as the water gets low in the soil. It will, therefore, be seen that a dry summer and autumn conduce to fevers, while a wet summer and autumn increase bowel affections. In a dry season the earth cracks in consequence of the evaporation of the water it contains, and with this evaporation are set free gases that are contained in the soil, in addition to the decomposition of vegetable matter, the necessary result of the atmosphere and light coming in contact with it.† These conditions do not obtain when the ground is covered or saturated with water.

---

* Zeitschrift für Biologie, 1865.

† The normal quantity of carbonic acid contained in the atmosphere is 1.4 volumes per 1000, but the air in the soil contains a large quantity, derived by absorption, or the action of rain, and in an enriched soil like ours, more largely from the decay of vegetation. It has been found to amount to 10, and even 20 per cent. In addition to the carbonic acid, there is also carburetted hydrogen. Cultivation of the soil, in the immediate vicinity of the city, would cause the consumption of these gases by vegetation, and therefore, would materially assist in rendering them innoxious in dry weather, when their escape into the atmosphere is most marked upon health.

INFANTILE DISEASES.
1866.

	January.	February.	March.	April.	May.	June.	July.	August.	September.	October.	November.	December.	TOTAL.
Cholera Infantum	....	....	2	....	1	4	194	212	95	47	6	1	592
Convulsions	24	23	17	23	23	26	59	37	22	46	47	36	380
Marasmus	....	....	1	....	1	2	1	....	5	3	1	1	15
Measles	....	....	2	4	7	18	67	47	14	6	1	....	166
Teething	8	4	3	5	14	11	30	37	26	18	7	3	166
Whooping Cough	1	2	....	1	3	6	15	63	40	19	17	17	184
TOTAL	33	29	25	33	49	67	366	424	202	139	79	58	1503

1867.

	January.	February.	March.	April.	May.	June.	July.	August.	September.	October.	November.	December.	TOTAL.
Cholera Infantum	....	....	....	....	5	....	....	192	212	84	41	4	538
Convulsions	38	18	43	20	39	31	36	23	26	43	27	41	389
Marasmus	2	1	....	....	1	3	25	29	27	13	9	6	116
Measles	....	....	1	1	3	8	11	17	10	4	8	24	87
Teething	12	9	12	6	5	4	15	40	23	14	5	3	148
Whooping Cough	1	4	11	10	4	4	6	6	2	1	3	....	62
TOTAL	53	38	60	43	58	50	283	332	176	116	54	77	1340

1868.

	January.	February.	March.	April.	May.	June.	July.	August.	September.	October.	November.	December.	TOTAL.
Cholera Infantum	....	2	1	....	1	8	284	280	143	17	2	1	739
Convulsions	51	41	42	29	36	43	90	74	76	39	44	40	605
Marasmus	7	9	4	5	7	6	19	39	27	14	10	11	158
Measles	21	24	21	12	5	12	7	2	3	1	2	3	113
Teething	6	5	1	7	11	4	33	44	46	23	6	4	190
Whooping Cough	3	1	1	2	....	6	13	15	16	12	8	7	64
TOTAL	88	82	70	55	60	79	446	454	311	106	72	66	1889

OLD AGE.

	Jan.	Feby.	Mar.	April	May.	June.	July.	Aug.	Sept.	Oct.	Nov.	Dec.	Tot'l.
1866	11	9	5	9	6	12	13	15	13	13	12	15	133
1867	6	9	8	5	6	9	3	4	3	4	5	5	67
1868	4	1	8	7	3	3	8	6	8	11	10	5	74
TOTAL	21	19	21	21	15	24	24	25	24	28	27	25	274

Extremes of heat and cold are necessarily destructive to infantile life and old age. Of all diseases to which children are subject, none is so fatal as Cholera Infantum. The number reported for 1866 is evidently below what it should be, while the nomenclature and reporting for 1867 are more accurate. The intensely hot weather, together with the rain, caused the fearful mortality of 1868, mostly in the undrained wards of the city. The mortality by Convulsions may be regarded as a sure index of the influence of climate on children. The epidemic tendency of 1866 is also shown, with the influence of extreme cold in increasing mortality, compared with the other years. Marasmus was imperfectly reported in 1866. The mortality by teething will give a better idea of climatic influences, and the same may be said with regard to Whooping Cough. The infantile mortality during the intensely hot weather of July, August, and September, was very great.

It will also be seen that the aged suffered severely in 1866, but the greater number of deaths reported in the first six months of 1867 as compared with the last, incline me to the opinion that the great difference in the two years is owing partially to the naming of the diseases, and the absence of any epidemic tendency in 1868, and also the fact that the aged can protect themselves better from the effect of cold than children.

From the foregoing, it must not be inferred that the general health of Chicago is bad, but, on the contrary, it compares favorably with any large city in the country; and I think it is not presuming too much to say that the climate of Chicago may be materially modified, and rendered more equable,* by the proper location of parks, and the planting of trees,† thereby diminishing the mortality of preventable diseases, and improving the general health. ‡

---

* The following facts illustrate the influence of equable temperature upon the mortality by pulmonary diseases; 1868, January, highest temperature 41, lowest 4, range 45, and mean temperature 20.3, deaths 145 ; 1869, January, highest temperature 51, lowest 17, range 34, and mean temperature 34.3, deaths 104 ; 1868, February, highest temperature 56, lowest -9, range 65, mean, 27.6, deaths 138 ; 1869, February, highest temperature 65, lowest 5, range 60, mean, 31.7, deaths 100.

† The environs of Chicago are for the most part destitute of trees, and when we consider the important part which they play in the economy of nature, it will appear obvious to every one that tree-planting would not only break the force of the wind, supply warmth in winter, and coolness in summer, and thus moderate the extremes of temperature, but at the same time absorb to a considerable extent, the noxious gases which are generated in every populous city,—supplying oxygen, and thus contributing to the public health. Trees should be planted in every street in the city, and on all the highways leading out of it, especially those running north and south; and should they at any time become too thick, they can easily be thinned out. What a blessing it would be, and at the same time what an ornament, if the right of way to every railroad leading out of Chicago, was devoted to tree-culture ! In winter they would serve as barriers against the drifting snows, diminish the amount of fuel necessary to propel the trains, and in summer they would afford a grateful shade. So intimately are trees associated with man, and so much do they contribute to his happiness and comfort, that their culture should everywhere be encouraged. " Persons are sometimes prevented from planting trees, on account of the slowness of their growth. What a mistake this is ! It is a strange feeling to feel — a strange complaint to utter—that any one thing in this world, animate or inanimate, is of too slow growth, for the nearer to its perfection, the nearer to its decay." " Let each young man plant trees that he may have something ever near to bring back pleasing recollections of his youth,— something, when he is an old man, that will seem of his own age, and sympathise with him, and look on him with a familiar face, that he may not feel quite alone among a new generation. Let the old man plant trees, they will keep him alive in the minds of men, the memory of one who lived not for himself."

‡ The location of Lincoln Park is all that could be desired, serving to protect the city from the north-east wind in spring. A park in the north-western part of the city is needed, extending from Chicago Avenue north, as a protection from the bleak north-west winds in winter and spring ; and, also,

INFLUENCE OF PARKS ON THE MIND.

We have thus far been considering the influence of parks and trees on the physical development; we now propose to call attention to their influence on the mental condition. In fact, such is the intimate connection between the two, that they cannot well be separated, as a sound and vigorous mind is generally dependent upon a healthy condition of the bodily organs, and without either, the object of life is but imperfectly attained. Juvenal, long ago, declared that, "*Sana mens in sano corpore*"—a sound mind in a sound body—should be the aspiration of every one. "Health of mind, as well as of body, is not only productive in itself of a greater sum of enjoyment than arises from other sources, but is the only condition of our frame in which we are capable of receiving pleasure from without."* In order, therefore, to preserve the mind from impairment of its energies and the derangement of its functions, physical exercise, as well as relaxation and recreation is necessary.

We live in an atmosphere of excitement, more so, perhaps, than any other community in the world, and it is therefore more necessary that all prudent safeguards should be thrown around us to prevent the impairment of the vigor of the mind and the inroads of disease.

We have neither leisure nor inclination to bestow many thoughts upon schemes much beyond the circle of our ordinary pursuits, and our happiness consists chiefly in the accumulation of wealth, and the accomplishment of something that is bold and novel. The sources of gratification are too few to furnish much relief to the excitement of our daily life, and our social intercourse is limited to the same necessities.

This is an age of great mental activity, and nowhere is the mind more stimulated than in Chicago. While it is true that the judicious

---

one in the south-western part of the city, extending from 16th or 22d Street to or beyond the city limits south, to moderate, so far as relates to the south-west winds, the extremes of heat and cold, in winter and summer, and to absorb the miasmatic exhalations of Mud Lake and the country adjoining the Illinois and Michigan Canal. A park should also be located south-east of the city, to protect it against the exhalations of the Calumet swamps, and the depressing effect of the wind from that direction. A careful examination of the topography of the localities indicated, will reveal the fact, in addition to the other reasons named, that the ground is low, and the surface drainage is bad, and that the location of the parks will obviate this objection, while, at the same time, the lands will cost less than if taken at other places, and that they will be more acceptable to all, than if differently placed. In other words, for sanitary and economical considerations, and for purposes of convenience, they are best. There is no city in the world, with the same population, where the immediate surroundings are so illy improved, as Chicago. The location of the parks in these directions would stimulate the improvement and cultivation of the soil, which fact, alone, would act beneficently in a sanitary point of view, but it would also create a demand for the manure and offal of the city, and thus indirectly assist in improving the public health, by the removal of offensive materials, while the cost to citizens and the city would be less than it now is.

* Sir James Mackintosh.

use of an organ, increases its power and confirms its health ; but excessive exercise which requires an undue share of vital energy, leads to an unhealthy condition.

"Much of the mental activity that characterizes our people," says a distinguished writer, "arises from the abundant opportunities that are offered for the pursuit of wealth, and the consequent variety and novelty of the enterprises undertaken for this purpose. All are hoping and striving to make or greatly to advance their fortunes, by some happy stroke of skill, some nicely balanced combination of chances, or some daring speculation. The result, all can see and admire, but few know anything of the wear and tear of mind by which it was achieved. Indeed, our ways of doing business, our notions of property, our ideas of happiness, all indicate, as strongly as traits of character can, that a large portion of our fellow citizens habitually live and move and have their being under an extraordinary pressure of excitement that brooks neither failure or delay. If unsuccessful in one attempt, our inexhaustible resources furnish the means and opportunities of trying another, while misfortune and disappointment stimulate rather than depress the mental energies."[*]

With how much truth and force can these remarks be applied to the inhabitants of our city, and their force is but too apparent in the rapid consumption of the mental powers, and the tendency to diseases of this character.[†]

This is not alone the result of diseases of the mind, but of others, particularly consumption, as will be seen by an examination of a table found elsewhere, where the deaths of males during the speculative excitement of 1856, and the consequent financial revulsion of 1857 and 1858, greatly exceed those of females, and, also, in the first years of the war of the Rebellion : and, no doubt, such was also the result of the depressing effect of the cholera on the mind, in increasing the mortality by this disease, during the last half of 1866 and the first half of 1867.

---

[*] Ray, *Mental Hygiene.*

[†] Owing to the different spheres in which the two sexes move, the effects of an undue exercise of the mental powers are more apparent in the male sex, as is evidenced by the following statement : Since July 1st, 1851, 179 males, and 77 females, have died of apoplexy : 363 males, and 267 females, of dropsy of the brain ; 1.613 males, and 1,308 females, of convulsions (nothing unusual in this difference of the sexes, as more males are born, and there is a greater mortality among males in infancy) ; epilepsy, 29 males, and 16 females ; palsy, 93 males, and 58 females. In apoplexy, epilepsy, and palsy, a better idea may be formed of the effect of the great mental activity that characterizes our people, although there is no doubt that we have an excess of males in this city. My confidence in the statistics, I must confess, is not what it should be, as, during the period in which they were reported, no less than 3,766 deaths are ascribed to unknown causes. This will, however, be better appreciated by the statistics of those who have died of old age during the same period. Of these there were, males, 359, and females, 398. The mortality should be about the same, owing to the fact that we have always had a larger male population than female, giving due credit for the greater female longevity.

We do not seem to appreciate that the highest degree of health is necessary to insure the most complete success, nor the importance of the maxim "*Festina lente.*" We need not be in such haste. Our climatic, independent of our geographical, position gives us vast advantages over our rivals, and it is a well established fact in European civilization, that climate has exercised the greatest influence on the physical and intellectual development of man.* We, perhaps more than any other community, need all the possible safeguards against over-work to be thrown around us, and I know of no better way than by the creation of parks, that will be an ornament to the city, and places of resort, where all may enjoy themselves in a rational and healthful manner. We need parks to induce out-door exercise, and for the pleasant influences connected with them, which are so beneficial to our over-worked business men, to dyspeptics, to those afflicted with nervous diseases, and, particularly, to the consumptive.†

* Buckle's *History of Civilization.*

† Contrary to the received opinion, I find, upon careful investigation, that the mortality by Consumption is not as great here as in nearly all the other large cities of the United States. It has been estimated that about one-sixth of all the deaths among the human race occurs from this disease, and that of 2,771,728 deaths from all diseases, between 1804 and 1860, 483,728 deaths, or 1 in 57, were caused by Consumption. [Dr. H. B. Millard.] In Boston the mortality is great, and not much change in the rate has taken place, while in New York the deaths have steadily diminished. Females are more liable than males, no doubt owing to their leading more sedentary lives. It has been found that the disease is less apt to be developed in rural districts, and that the liability to it is increased by want of exercise and confined air. The important part that parks exercise over this disease will, therefore, be appreciated, in the inducements they offer to exercise in the open air. The following table will show the mortality of Chicago, and other cities.

DEATHS BY CONSUMPTION FROM JULY 1ST, 1851, TO JANUARY 1ST, 1869.

	Males.	Females.	Total.	Population.	One Death in	Excess of Males over Females.
Six Months, 1851	23	18	41	39,685	484	5
Year of 1852	63	49	112	49,407	441	14
" " 1853	103	64	167	59,130	354	39
" " 1854	104	91	195	69,565	357	13
" " 1855	91	63	154	80,000	519	28
" " 1856	174	112	286	84,113	294	62
" " 1857	145	108	253	92,113	364	37
" " 1858	196	133	329	96,363	293	63
" " 1859	127	120	247	101,780	412	7
" " 1860	144	128	272	109,260	402	16
" " 1861	196	120	316	123,623	391	76
" " 1862	203	146	349	138,186	396	57
" " 1863	136	131	267	153,769	576	5
" " 1864	216	195	411	169,353	412	21
" " 1865	189	147	336	178,492	531	42
" " 1866	226	180	406	200,418	493	46
" " 1867	223	181	404	225,326	557	42
" " 1868	238	180	418	252,054	603	58
	2,797	2,166	4,963			631

Average Excess of Males over Females.

First nine years ....30 per annum.
Last " " ....40 " "

We need parks for our school children, as we have no places to which they can resort for out-of-door play, and where they can obtain healthful recreation, with the exception of the limited grounds surrounding the school houses. They can also be made use of as the means of instruction, by the arboretum, botanical collections and the collections of animals that are found in them.

The moral influence of parks is decided. Man is brought in contact with nature,—is taken away from the artificial conditions in which he lives in cities ; and such associations exercise a vast influence for good. In the Central Park, only 568 arrests have been made, and these of a trivial character, out of 30,731,847 visitors. "*The people of Baltimore have been their own conservators of the parks. They appreciate and enjoy them, and they preserve them. The appeal made to them by the commission in the first year of the parks, has been most fully and honorably responded to.*" * We have no places of resort on holidays. By creating them, we take many away from other and worse places, and thus do much toward encouraging the young in habits of sobriety and temperance. They also afford a field for the exercise of those robust games which tend so much to the development of the physical system.

From the preceding observations, particularly on the local topography and character of the diseases, there ought to be little doubt as to the proper positions in which parks should be located, in order to make them alike convenient to the city, and promotive of the public health.

There is upon this question a community of interest between the different sections of the city, which ought to override all considerations of a local nature, and lead to harmonious action. All should coöperate to give each section the full benefits of such public resorts, bearing in mind, that while one portion of the city may be locally favored, the entire population share in the advantages. While one portion of the city may be peculiarly exposed to malaria, the

---

Average Excess of Males over Females, compared with Population.

First nine years..1 in 2489 of Population.
Last   "   "   ....1 in 4291 "   "

Average Proportion of Deaths by Consumption.

First nine years..1 in 367 of deaths from all causes.
Last   "   "   ....1 in 484 "   "   "   "   "

Philadelphia, 1862, 1 in 7 7·9, or 13 per cent ; 1863, 1 in 7 2·3 or 13 per cent. ; 1864, 1 in 7 5·8, or 13 per cent. ; 1867, 1 in 6 1·2, or 15 1·2 per cent. New Orleans, 1867, 1 in 15, or 6 6·10 per cent. St. Louis, Mo., 1868, 1 in 10 1·3, or 9 7·10 per cent. Providence, R. I., 1866, 1 in 5 1·7, or 19 4·10 per cent. Chicago, 1868, 1 in 14 1·3, or 7 per cent. New York, 1867, 12 per cent.

* Ninth Annual Report Park Commission.

subtle and invisible influence may be wafted to the remotest parts, abated in virulence, but still pestiferous.

In this connection, we may use the language of Lucretius, in reference to the plague :

> "When first the air, surcharged with poisonous power,
> Moves far remote, we deem it but a mist,
> Or floating cloud ; but having reached our midst,
> Distils throughout its course a fatal dew
> Which blights and kills."

During the past season, in July, the south-east wind blew for several days, carrying with it the exhalations of the Calumet swamps and diffusing them over the entire city, causing a marked mortality in the Twelfth ward. The south-west wind is the prevailing one, as we have seen, during the summer and autumn months, and the mortality, for the past year, was greater in the Thirteenth ward than in the Fifth, where, so far as relates to drainage, cleanliness, comforts of living, &c., the conditions are far inferior.

Regarding, then, this question in a comprehensive view, it may be affirmed that the benefits to be derived from the location of parks are not of a local, but general character, and such as should enlist, in their establishment, the efforts of every citizen who has the welfare of the city at heart.

Park Acts.

NORTH CHICAGO.

AN ACT TO FIX THE BOUNDARIES OF LINCOLN PARK IN THE CITY OF CHICAGO, AND PROVIDE FOR ITS IMPROVEMENT.

SECTION 1. *Be it enacted by the People of the State of Illinois, represented in the General Assembly:* That all of the land situate and lying within the following boundaries, to-wit: Commencing at the intersection of North avenue in the city of Chicago and county of Cook with Lake Michigan, and running thence west along said North avenue to North Clark street; thence along North Clark street to North Franklin street; thence along North Franklin street to Fullerton avenue; thence along Fullerton avenue to the west line of the southeast quarter of section 28 in township 40, north of range 14 east of the third principal meridian; thence along said west line to the northwest corner of said southeast quarter of section 28; thence along the north line of said southeast quarter to Lake Michigan; and thence along the shore of Lake Michigan at low water mark, as the same now is or hereafter may be, to the place of beginning—be, and the same is hereby, declared to be a public park, to be known as Lincoln Park, and shall be deemed to have been taken by the city of Chicago for public use and for a public park.

SEC. 2. All of said land now belonging to the city of Chicago shall be and is hereby appropriated for such park without any compensation to the city, and the title of any of said land not now owned by the city may be acquired by said city by purchase or condemnation as herein provided. The Board of Commissioners of Lincoln Park, as hereinafter created, may purchase any of said lands at fair and reasonable prices, to be determined by them and paid for out of bonds or money coming to their hands for the purpose of acquiring the title thereto, and the same shall be conveyed to and vest in the city, to be used as a part of the park, or the same may be acquired in the manner hereinafter set forth.

SEC. 3. Three discreet and competent freeholders, citizens of Chicago, shall be appointed by the circuit court of Cook county, within three months after the passage of this act, and on application of the Board of Commissioners of said park, to act as appraisers in relation to the taking and the value of said lands mentioned in the first section of this act or any part thereof, and in case of the death, resignation, disqualification or refusal to act of either of said appraisers, it shall be lawful for the said circuit court, at any general or special term thereof, on application of said Board of Commissioners, and from time to time, as often as said event shall happen, to appoint any other discreet or disinterested person, being a citizen of the city of Chicago, in the place of said appraisers so dying, resigning or refusing to act, and said appraisers shall proceed to discharge the duties of their appointment, and to complete their estimate and awards, as soon as conveniently may be, and shall file their final report in the office of the clerk of the circuit court of Cook county within three months of the date of their appointment.

Sec. 4. It shall be competent and lawful for a majority of of said Board of Appraisers, designated as aforesaid, to perform the trust and duties of their appointment; and their acts shall be as valid and effectual as the acts of all the appraisers so to be appointed, if they had acted therein, would have been. And in every case the proceedings and decisions of a majority in number of said Board of Appraisers, acting in the premises shall be as valid and effectual as if the said appraisers appointed for such purposes had all concurred and joined therein.

Sec. 5. The appraisers herein provided for in relation to the taking and the value of any of the lands mentioned in the first section of this act, shall make just and true estimate of the value of such lands and of the loss and damage to the respective owners, lessees and parties and persons respectively entitled to or interested in the same, together with the tenements, hereditaments and appurtenances, privileges or advantages to the same belonging or in any wise appertaining, by and in consequence of the relinquishing the same to the said city of Chicago; and in making said estimate they shall not make any deduction or allowance for any supposed advantages to be derived from taking said lands as public places or in consequence thereof; and the amounts so estimated, when duly confirmed, shall be paid as hereinafter in this act provided. Whenever such estimate shall be completed, they shall file the same with the clerk of the circuit court of Cook county, and thereupon proceedings may be had to correct or confirm the same as in this act provided.

Sec. 6. Said appraisers and any party being the owner of, or interested in, any of the lands mentioned in this act, may agree upon the value thereof and upon the amount of damages and compensation to be awarded therefor, and said appraisers may make special reports in relation to any matter so agreed upon, and any such special report may be filed and proceedings may be had to confirm the same, and the same may be confirmed in the same manner and with like effect, as is provided herein with relation to other reports of said appraisers; and upon the confirmation of any such special report, the amount of the awards thus confirmed shall be paid in the same manner as if such awards had been made in a general report of said appraisers and duly confirmed.

Sec. 7. Before proceeding to discharge any of their duties the appraisers shall respectively take and subscribe an oath in writing before some officer authorized by law to administer oaths, honestly and faithfully to discharge the duties which may devolve upon them, in pursuance of this act, which oath shall be filed in the office of the clerk of the county court of the county of Cook. Said appraisers shall proceed as soon as may be after their appointment to discharge the duties of their trust, and to make and complete their estimates and awards, and reports, as hereinafter provided, and every estimate, award and report so made, shall be signed by at least a majority of said appraisers, and filed in the office of the circuit court of the county of Cook, and notice thereof given to the counsel for the corporation of the said city of Chicago, within ten days after receiving such notice of the filing of any report of such Board of Appraisers, said Corporation Counsel shall give notice by publication for ten days, in at least two daily papers of the said city of Chicago, that he will, at a term of said circuit court designated therein, and at the time and place to be designated, in said notice, present said report for confirmation. And if said Corporation Counsel shall not, within the time prescribed, cause such notice to be given, and the report to be presented for confirmation, then such notice may be given, and said report may be presented for confirmation, as above described, by said appraisers, or by any party whose lands are to be taken, and to whom compensation is estimated and awarded by such report. It shall be the duty of said court, at the time mentioned in said notice, to proceed immediately to the hearing of said report, and it shall have priority over all other causes pending in said court. The said court shall pronounce judgment on said report, and shall confirm the same against the several lots or parcels of land described in said report in respect to which no objections shall be filed, and such judgment shall be a lawful and sufficient condemnation of the lands and property appropriated and sought to be condemned and not objected to; and the court shall hear and determine all objections in a summary way, without pleadings, and shall and may, on such hearing, when objections have been interposed, render such judgment as shall seem proper, modifying and changing such assessment as it shall deem proper, and any appeal therefrom shall not invalidate or affect said judgment, or delay the same except as to the property described in said appeal. Such judgment, as far as not appealed from, shall be a lawful and sufficient condemnation of the lands and property appropriated, and any appeal shall not delay the proceedings under said judgment, except as to the property described in said appeal.

SEC. 8. Payment of the damages awarded in and by the judgments entered as aforesaid shall be made immediately, and the Board of Park Commissioners, as hereinafter appointed, may either pay such damage to the person appearing to be entitled to the same, or bring into the said circuit court and deposit with the clerk thereof the amount of such damage, specifying at the time of each deposit, in a written report, to be made to said court, the several pieces of land condemned, and which are paid for by said deposit, and upon payment being made as aforesaid, the said lands shall vest forever in the said city of Chicago for the purposes and uses in this act mentioned.

SEC. 9. It shall be the duty of any person or persons owning cemetery lots included within the lands in the first section of this act described and to be condemned by said commissioners, to remove any bodies that may be therein interred, within six months of the confirmation of so much of the report of said commissioners as relates to said lots; and if said removal shall not be made within six months, the Board of Park Commissioners may, at any time thereafter, make such removal.

Sec. 10. The appraisers shall also, as a part of Lincoln Park, lay out a drive two hundred feet wide (so the east line shall be the waters of Lake Michigan), from Pine street to the south line of said park, and shall proceed to make an assessment for the payment of the land taken for the same, according to the provisions of the charter of the city of Chicago, in staking lands for the opening of a street, and shall file their report with the clerk of the circuit court, when the same proceedings shall be had as provided in this act in regard to the lands to be taken for the park. The said circuit court may render judgment against the lands and lots assessed for the several amounts assessed for benefits remaining unpaid, and the collection thereof shall be made and enforced, as is the case for the collection for taxes, and the money so collected shall be paid to the Park Commissioners, and by them paid to the several persons entitled to damages for lands taken for such drive.

Sec. 11. Such drive, when thus laid out, shall be a part of said Lincoln Park, and shall be under the control and management of the Board of Commissioners to the same extent as herein provided in reference to said park, and it shall be improved by the same means.

Sec. 12. For the purpose of paying for the land taken for such park, under the provisions of this act, the bonds of the city of Chicago, to such an amount as shall be necessary for that purpose, shall be issued by the Mayor, Comptroller and Clerk of said city, from time to time, as the same shall be required by the Board of Park Commissioners for the purpose aforesaid, and shall be delivered to said board upon demand, and said bonds shall be payable twenty years from the date thereof, and shall bear interest at the rate of seven per cent. per annum, payable half yearly on the first days of January and July, in each year; and the said bonds, and the proceeds of the sale thereof, shall constitute the fund for paying the cost of the lands taken for the park.

Sec. 13. As said bonds shall from time to time issue, the comptroller shall cause to be kept in his office, in a book to be provided for that purpose, a true and correct statement and account of each and every bond by him executed, showing the number of each bond, and the date and amount thereof, and the time when due (and said books shall be open for public inspection), and which books shall be delivered by him to his successor in office. The comptroller shall take a receipt from the person authorized by said board to receive said bonds.

Sec. 14. The bonds of the city of Chicago, which shall be issued by virtue of this act, may be used by said Board of Commissioners at their par value, by paying any amount which said city shall have become liable to pay for such lands purchased or condemned under this act, or the same may be sold at public or private sale, or subscription, upon such terms as said commissioners shall determine; and the said Board of Park Commissioners may pledge any of said bonds for money borrowed temporarily, at an ordinary rate of interest, not exceeding 10 per cent. per annum, if they shall deem it necessary and expedient so to do.

SEC. 15. The Board of Park Commissioners shall cause a full description of the bonds received from the city, to be entered in a record, to be provided for that purpose, which shall show the date, number and amount of each bond, the time when received, the time when and to whom sold, and the amount received therefor, and shall, on or before the 1st day of April in each year, furnish a copy thereof, verified by the oath of the custodian of such records, to the city comptroller.

SEC. 16. The property of the city of Chicago, and the lands authorized to be taken by this act for a public park, are hereby pledged for the payment of the principal and interest of said bonds.

SEC. 17. The Board of Park Commissioners hereinafter mentioned, is hereby authorized, and it shall be their duty, on or before the first day of October in each year, to fix upon the amount, not exceeding $75,000, that may be necessary to be expended for the improvement and repair of said park and drive during the next succeeding year, and certify the same to the clerk of the county court of Cook county, and said clerk shall apportion said amount upon the taxable property returned by the Assessors of North Chicago and Lake View, and compute the same as part of the taxes due and payable by the owners of said property set down or described in a separate column headed "Lincoln Park Tax," and the same shall be included in the warrant issued for the collection of taxes, and collected as other taxes. In case of a failure to pay the same, judgment may be rendered against the real estate assessed, and the like proceedings had as for other taxes. The taxes so collected shall be paid to the park commissioners, and used by them in improving and keeping in repair the park and drive.

SEC. 18. The appraisers appointed by virtue of this act, shall have authority to employ surveyors, and to use any map or file belonging to said city or to said county of Cook, and to cause maps to be made as may be necessary, and said appraisers shall be allowed a compensation of five dollars per day for their time actually employed in discharging their duty as such appraisers, and all such compensation and the necessary expenses in discharging their duties, shall be allowed and taxed by the court aforesaid, and paid by said city of Chicago, and shall be added to and become a part of the cost of said park.

SEC. 19. The said Lincoln Park shall be under the exclusive control of a Board of Commissioners to consist of five persons, who shall be named and styled the Commissioners of Lincoln Park. A majority of said commissioners (in office for the time being), shall constitute a quorum for the transaction of business; but no action of said board shall be final or binding until it shall receive the approval of a majority of said board, whose names shall be recorded in its minutes.

SEC. 20. E. B. McCagg, John B. Turner, Andrew Nelson, Joseph Stockton and Jacob Rehm, are hereby appointed and shall constitute the first Board of Commissioners of Lincoln Park. They shall hold office as such commissioners for five years. No member of such board shall receive any compensation for his services. In case of a vacancy within said five years, the same may be filled by the remaining members of said board, and all vacancies occasioned by the expiration of the term of office, shall be filled by the judge of the circuit court of Cook county.

SEC. 21. The said board shall have full and exclusive power to govern, manage and direct the said park; to lay out and regulate the same; to pass ordinances for the regulation and government thereof; to appoint such engineers, surveyors and other officers, except a police force, as may be necessary; to prescribe and define their respective duties and authority; to fix the amount of their compensation, and to require bonds for the faithful performance of their duties; and generally, in regard to said park, shall possess all the power and authority now by law conferred on or possessed by the common council of said city in respect to public squares and places in said city. They may vacate any public street or alley within the limits of said park, and shall lay out a street not exceeding one hundred feet, and not less than eighty feet in width, north from Fullerton avenue, along the west line of said park to the northern boundary thereof, and may exercise the same power and control over such street as the rest of the park.

SEC. 22. It shall be a misdemeanor for any commissioner to be directly or indirectly in any way pecuniarily interested in any contract, or work of any kind whatever, connected with said park; and it shall be the duty of any commissioner, or other person who may have any knowledge or information of the violation of this provision, forthwith to report the same to the mayor of the city of Chicago, who shall present the facts of the case to the judge of the circuit court of Cook county. Such judge shall hear in a summary manner such commissioner in relation thereto, and if after such hearing he shall be satisfied of the truth thereof, he shall immediately remove the commissioner thus offending, subject to a fine and imprisonment. Every commissioner shall, before entering upon the duties of his office, take and subscribe an oath faithfully to perform the duties of his office, which oath shall be filed in the office of the said clerk of the circuit court of the county of Cook, and shall each give a bond in the penal sum of fifty thousand dollars for the faithful performance of his duty, and payable to the city of Chicago.

SEC. 23. Said Board of Commissioners for the government of said park shall, in the month of April of each year, make to the common council of said city, a full report of their proceedings and a detailed statement of all their receipts and expenses, under oath. It shall be the duty of said commissioners to let all amounts exceeding in amount twenty-five hundred dollars, by contract, in the manner provided in the charter of the city of Chicago for letting the contracts for public improvements.

SEC. 24. It shall be lawful for the commissioners of said park to let, from year to year, any building, and the grounds attached thereto, belonging to said city, which may be within the limits of said city, until the same shall be required for the laying out and regulation thereof, when the said buildings shall be removed, except such as may be used for the purposes of such park. The said commissioners may sell any building or other material, being within the limits of said park and belonging to said city, which, in their judgment, shall not be required for the purposes of said park, or for public use, and the proceeds of which shall be deposited to the credit of said commissioners, and devoted to the improvement of the park

SEC. 25. None of the said commissioners, nor any persons, whether in the employ of the said commissioners or otherwise, shall have the power to create any debt, obligation, claim or liability for or on account of said board, or the monies or properties under his control, except with the express authority of said board, conferred at a meeting thereof duly convened and held.

SEC. 26. The office of either the said commissioners who shall not attend the meetings of said board for three successive months, after having been duly notified of said meetings, without reason therefor satisfactory to the said board, or without leave of absence from said board, may be by said board declared vacant.

SEC. 27. It shall be lawful for the said Board of Commissioners at any meeting thereof, duly convened, to pass such ordinances as they may deem necessary for the regulation, use, and government of the park under their charge, not inconsistent with the provisions of this act. Such ordinances shall immediately, upon their passage, be published for ten days, in two daily papers in said city.

SEC. 28. The persons offending against said ordinances shall be deemed guilty of a misdemeanor, and shall be punished, on conviction, before any court of competent jurisdiction in the county of Cook, by a fine not exceeding one thousand dollars, or by imprisonment, or both, in the discretion of the court.

SEC. 29. Real and personal property may be granted, bequeathed or conveyed to said city of Chicago, for the purpose of the improvement or ornamentation of said park, or for the establishment or maintenance, within the limits of said park, of museums, zoological, or other gardens, collections of natural history or works of art, upon such trusts and conditions as may be prescribed by the grantors and donors thereof, and agreed to by said Board of Park Commissioners; and all property so devised, granted, bequeathed or conveyed, and the rents, issues, profit and income thereof, shall be subject to the exclusive management, direction and control of the commissioners of the park.

SEC. 30. This act shall take effect from and after its passage.

Approved Feb. 8, 1869.

— — — —

SOUTH CHICAGO.

ACT TO PROVIDE FOR THE LOCATION AND MAINTENANCE OF A PARK FOR THE TOWNS OF SOUTH CHICAGO, HYDE PARK AND LAKE.

SECTION 1. *Be it enacted by the People of the State of Illinois, represented in the General Assembly*: That five persons, who shall be appointed by the Governor of the State of Illinois, together with their successors, be, and they are hereby constituted a Board of Public Park Commissioners, for the towns of South Chicago, Hyde Park, and Lake, to be known under the name of The South Park Commissioners; and in case of the failure of any of said persons to accept such appointment, and to qualify thereunder as hereinafter provided, within sixty days after the passage of this act, the place of such person in said commission shall be thereby vacated, and it shall be the duty of a majority of the commissioners so accepting, to appoint some suitable person to fill the place thus made vacant, which appointment, when accepted by such nominee, shall constitute such person a commissioner under this act. And a majority of said commissioners shall so continue to nominate until the board shall consist of five persons. Each of said commissioners, before entering upon the duties of his office, shall take an oath to well and properly discharge the duties of his office for the interests of the public, which oaths shall be reduced to writing, subscribed to by him, and filed in the office of the county clerk of Cook county. They shall each give a bond in the penal sum of fifty thousand dollars, with one or more sureties, to be approved of by the judge of the circuit court of Cook county, to the treasurer of Cook county, conditioned for the faithful discharge of their duties under this act.

Sec. 2. As soon as convenient after the said board shall be constituted as aforesaid, the members thereof shall decide by lot, at a meeting to be called by any three of them, as to the respective term for which each member shall hold his office; the number of lots shall equal the number of commissioners, and the person drawing the longest term shall serve for five years from the first day of March, A. D. 1869; the one drawing the next, shall serve for four years from said date; the one drawing the next, shall serve for three years from said date; and so on until the term of each one of said commissioners shall be definitely determined, each one serving for the length of time inscribed on the lot drawn by him—the last of said commissioners serving for the term of one year only from said first day of March, A. D. 1869. As soon as the term of office of each of said commissioners shall be determined as aforesaid, said board shall organize by electing one of their number as president, and one of their number as auditor; they shall also appoint a treasurer, prescribe his duties, and fix his compensation, who shall give bond for the faithful discharge of his duties in the penal sum of five hundred thousand dollars, with not less than three sufficient sureties, to be approved by the judge of the circuit court of Cook county. They shall also choose a secretary, who shall not necessarily be a commissioner, and who shall hold his office until his successor shall be appointed as hereinafter provided; and all officers appointed by the board shall be subject to removal at the pleasure of the board. The said board shall adopt a seal, and alter the same at pleasure; they shall keep a complete record of all their proceedings, which shall be open at all times for the inspection of the public. The said commissioners shall receive no compensation for their services, except the president, who may, in the discretion of said board, have and receive such compensation as may be fixed as hereinafter provided, not to exceed three thousand dollars per annum. All vacancies occurring in said board shall be filled by the appointment of the judge of the circuit court of Cook county, when such vacancy or vacancies shall occur. Said board of commissioners shall be a body politic and corporate, and shall have and enjoy all the powers necessary for the purposes of this act.

SEC. 3. The president, auditor, treasurer, and secretary, shall be elected annually by said board, at the annual meeting thereof, and shall receive such salary for their services as the said board shall from time to time determine, not exceeding, for each of said officers, the sum of three thousand dollars per annum.

SEC. 4. The said commissioners, by this act, are authorized and empowered to, and they shall within ninety days after their organization as aforesaid, or as soon thereafter as practicable, select the following described lands, situated in the towns of South Chicago, Hyde Park and Lake, in Cook county, Illinois, to wit: Commencing at the south-west corner of Fifty-first street and Cottage Grove avenue, running thence south along the west side of Cottage Grove avenue to the south line of Fifty-ninth street; thence east along the south line of Fifty-ninth street to the east line of Hyde Park avenue; thence north on Hyde Park avenue to Fifty-sixth street; thence east along the south line of Fifty-sixth street to Lake Michigan; thence southerly along the shore of the lake to a point due east of the center of section twenty-four (24), in township thirty-eight (38) north, range fourteen (14); thence west through the centre of said section twenty-four (24) to Hyde Park avenue; thence north on the east line of Hyde Park avenue to the north line of Sixtieth street, so called; thence west on the north line of Sixtieth street, so-called, to Kankakee avenue; thence north on the east line of Kankakee avenue to Fifty-first street; thence east to a point to the place of beginning; also, a piece of land commencing at the south-east corner of Kankakee avenue and Fifty-fifth street, running thence west a strip two hundred feet wide, adjoining the north line of Fifty-fifth street, along said Fifty-fifth street to the line between ranges thirteen (13) and (14) east; thence north, east of and adjoining said line, a strip two hundred feet wide, to the Illinois and Michigan canal; also, a parcel of land beginning at the south-west corner of Douglas place and Kankakee avenue, running thence south, a strip of land one hundred and thirty-two feet wide, along the west side of said Kankakee avenue, to a point one hundred and fifty feet south of the south line of Fifty-first street; also, a strip of land commencing at the intersection of Cottage Grove avenue and Fifty-first street, running thence east one hundred feet in width on each side of the center line of Fifty-first street, to a point one hundred feet east of the center line of Drexel avenue; also, a strip of land extending north from the intersection of Fifty-first street with Drexel avenue, one hundred feet in width, on each side of the center line of said avenue, to the north line of Forty-third street; thence northerly, a strip of land two hundred feet in width, till it meets or intersects with Elm street in Cleaverville; thence northerly along said Elm street, two hundred feet in width, west from the east line of said street, to its intersection with Oakland avenue; which said land and premises, when acquired by said commissioners as provided by this act, shall be held, managed and controlled by them and their successors, as

B

a public park, for the recreation, health and benefit of the public, and free to all persons forever, subject to such necessary rules and regulations as shall, from time to time, be adopted by said commissioners and their successors for the well ordering and government of the same.

SEC. 5. In case the said commissioners cannot agree with the owner or owners, lessees or occupants of any of the said real estate selected by them as aforesaid. they may proceed to procure the condemnation of the same, in the manner prescribed in the act of the General Assembly of the State of Illinois entitled "An act to amend the law condemning right of way for the purpose of internal improvement," approved June 22, 1852, and the acts amendatory thereof, the provisions of which said act, and the several acts amendatory thereof, are hereby extended to the park and park commissioners to be created by virtue of this act.

SEC. 6. When the title to the land selected for such park as herein provided shall have been acquired by said commissioners, by gift, condemnation, or otherwise, it shall be the duty of such commissioners to make, acknowledge, and file for record in the office of the recorder of deeds for Cook county, a map, showing the said land, with a correct description, including section, township and range.

SEC. 7. As soon as the amount required for the condemnation of the grounds selected for said park shall have been ascertained by said commissioners, with reasonable certainty, they shall apply to the judge of the circuit court of Cook county for the appointment of three freeholders of the county of Cook as park assessors. The commissioners shall give notice, in one or more of the daily newspapers published in the city of Chicago, of the time when such application will be made, and all parties interested may appear, and be heard by said Judge touching such appointment. At the time fixed for such application, the court, after hearing such persons as shall desire to be heard touching such appointment, shall nominate and appoint three assessors for the purposes provided in this act. The said assessors shall proceed to assess the amount so ascertained upon property in the towns of South Chicago, Hyde Park and Lake, in Cook county, deemed benefited by reason of the improvement occasioned by the location of said park, as near as may be in proportion to the benefits resulting thereto : *Provided*, that the aggregate of said benefits is equal to or greater than the amount of said damages; and in case the aggregate of the benefits is less than the damages, then the balance of the damages over the benefits shall be paid from the fund provided for in section eight of this act. Upon entering on the duties of their office, the said assessors shall make oath before the clerk of the said circuit court faithfully and impartially to discharge the duties of their office. They shall give at least ten days' notice, in one of the said daily papers, of the time and place of their meeting for the purpose of making said assessment, and may adjourn such meeting from time to time, until the same shall be completed. In making the said assessment, the said assessors shall estimate the value of the several lots, blocks, or parcels of land deemed benefited by them as aforesaid, and shall include the same, together with the amount assessed as benefits, in the assessment roll. All parties interested may appear before said assessors, and may be heard touching any matter connected with the assessment. When the same shall be completed, it shall be signed by the assessors, and returned to the said circuit court, and shall be filed by the clerk thereof. The assessors shall thereupon give at least ten days' notice, in one of the said daily papers, of the filing of said assessment roll, and that they will, on a day therein named, apply to the said circuit court for confirmation of the same, which said notice shall be published at least ten days before the time fixed for such application. Said circuit court shall have power to revise, correct, amend or confirm said assessment, in whole or in part, and may make or order a new assessment, in whole or in part. and the same revise and confirm. upon like notice. All parties interested may appear before said circuit court, either in person or by attorney, when such application shall be made, and may object to said assessment, either in whole or in part, provided all objections shall be in writing, and shall be filed at least three days before the time fixed for the application, and shall specify the lot, block, or parcels of land on behalf of which objection is made. After the confirmation of said assessment, the clerk of said circuit court shall file a copy thereof, under the seal of his said court, with the clerk of the county court of Cook county, and such assessment shall be a lien upon the several lots, blocks, or parcels of land assessed for benefits as aforesaid. Ten per cent. of the amount so ascertained shall be due and payable annually, and the clerk of said Cook county court shall include in the general tax warrants of each year, until the whole sum shall be paid, for the collection of State and county taxes in the said towns of South Chicago, Hyde Park and Lake, ten per cent. of the said assessments, in an appropriate column, to be termed "South Park Assessment," with the amount to be collected opposite the several lots, blocks, or parcels of land assessed as aforesaid; and like proceedings, in all respects, shall be had for enforcing the collection of the same as is now provided by law for the collection of state and county taxes. The money collected under the provision of this section shall be paid to the treasurer of Cook county, for which he and his sureties shall be responsible. as fully as for any other moneys by him received as treasurer of Cook county, and be held by him in the same manner, and be subject to the same control and direction, as provided in this act for other moneys belonging to said corporation; and the treasurer of Cook county shall be entitled to receive one-half of one per cent., and no more. of said moneys, as a full compensation for receiving and disbursing the same.

SEC. 8. For any deficiency arising through acquiring title to said park, and for the payment of the expenses of enclosing. maintaining and improving the park herein provided for, and the expenses. disbursements and charges in the premises. the said commissioners shall have power to loan or borrow, from time to time, for such time as they shall deem expedient, a sum of money not exceeding two millions of dollars, and shall have authority to issue bonds. secured upon the said park and improvements, which bonds shall issue under the seal of said commissioners, and shall be signed by said commissioners. and countersigned by the secretary of said board. and bear interest not exceeding seven per cent. per annum; and it shall be the duty of said commissioners to keep an accurate register of all bonds issued by them, showing the number, date and amount of each bond, and to whom the same was issued, and said register shall at all times be open to the investigation of the public; and for the payment of the principal and interest of said bonds the said park and improvements shall be irrevocably pledged, and the towns of South Chicago, Hyde Park and Lake shall be irrevocably bound; and said bonds may be sold by said commissioners upon such terms and for such prices as, in the judgment of said commissioners, can be obtained for the same in cash.

Sec. 9. The said board of park commissioners shall, annually, on or before the first day of December in each year, transmit to the clerk of the county court of Cook county an estimate, in writing, of the amount of money, not exceeding in any one year three hundred thousand dollars, necessary for the payment of the interest on the bonds issued by said board, and that, in addition thereto, will be required for the improvement, maintenance, and government of said park during the current year; and the said clerk shall proceed to determine what per cent. said sum is on the taxable property of said towns, according to the several assessors' returns for the respective year, and shall, in the next general tax warrants for the collection of state and county taxes in said several towns, set down the amount chargeable to the several persons, corporations, lots or parcels of ground, in a separate or appropriate column, and shall receive such compensation as now allowed by law; and the collectors, respectively, shall proceed to collect the same in the manner now provided by law for the collection of state and county taxes; and all the provisions of law, in respect to the collection of state and county taxes, and proceedings to enforce the same, so far as applicable, shall apply to said assessments and taxes. The said sum of money shall be placed by the treasurer of the said county of Cook to the credit of the said board of park commissioners, and shall be drawn by said board from the county treasury by warrant, signed by the president and secretary of the board, and countersigned by the auditor, to be appointed as aforesaid, and in no other way; the appointment of such auditor or comptroller having been first duly certified by such president and secretary, and filed in the office of said treasurer of Cook county.

Sec. 10. It shall be lawful for said commissioners to vacate and close up any and all public roads and highways, excepting railroads, which may pass through, divide, or separate any lands selected or appropriated by them for the purposes of a park; and no such road shall be laid out through said park except such as the said commissioners shall lay out and construct.

Sec. 11. No one of the said commissioners shall be interested, either directly or indirectly, in any contract entered into by them with any other person; nor shall they be interested, directly or indirectly, in the purchase of any material to be used or applied in and about the uses and purposes contemplated in this act. And it shall be a misdemeanor for any commissioner to be directly or indirectly interested, or in any way pecuniarily interested in any contract or work of any kind whatever, connected with said park.

SEC. 12. The said commissioners, or either of them, may be removed from office by the judge of the circuit court of Cook county, upon the petition presented to him in term time or in vacation, by one hundred free-holders of said towns of South Chicago, Hyde Park, and Lake, if it shall appear, after hearing and proof before said judge, that the said commissioners, or either of them, have been guilty of misdemeanor or malfeasance in office under this act; and if the said judge shall remove any two or more of said commissioners from office for any cause, before the expiration of their term of office, they are hereby empowered to appoint others in their stead, who shall fill such offices for and during the unexpired term of such commissioners so removed.

SEC. 13. The said board shall have the full and exclusive power to govern, manage, and direct said park; to lay out and regulate the same; to pass ordinances for the regulation and government thereof; to appoint such engineers, surveyors, clerks, and other officers, including a police force, as may be necessary; to define and prescribe their respective duties and authority; fix the amount of their compensation; and generally, in regard to said park, they shall possess all the power and authority now by law conferred upon or possessed by the common council of the city of Chicago, in respect to the public squares and places in said city; and it shall be lawful for them to commence the improvement of said park as soon as they have obtained one hundred acres of the premises herein described.

SEC. 14. The office of any commissioner under this act, who shall not attend meetings of the board for three successive months, after having been duly notified of said meetings, without leave of absence from said board, may, by said board, be declared vacant.

SEC. 15. The real estate and personal property of said corporation shall be exempted from taxation and assessment.

SEC. 16. All moneys belonging or to belong to any park fund now in existence or hereafter to be created, and all bonds, and the proceeds from sales thereof, now authorized or hereafter to be authorized to be issued by the city of Chicago for park purposes, in or to which the South Division of the city of Chicago may now or shall hereafter be entitled to a distributive share, shall be devoted and applied to the purchase or maintenance and improvement of the park contemplated and created by this act, under the direction and control of the commissioners provided for in this act.

SEC. 17. The bonds to be issued under this act may be received in payment of any assessment, whether such bond or assessment shall have become due or not, upon such terms as shall be fair, just and equitable; and upon the payment of any assessment, the land upon which the same is assessed shall be free from any lien or liability to pay the same; and such payment shall be reported to the county clerk of Cook county, and entered upon the record of the assessment.

SEC. 18. There shall be an election held in the towns of South Chicago, Hyde Park and Lake, on the fourth Tuesday of March next after the passage of this act, at which election the legal voters voting at such election shall vote for or against this act. The tickets shall be printed or written, "For

Park," or "Against Park;" and if a majority of the votes cast on the subject of park shall be "For Park," then this act shall take effect and be in force, but not otherwise. The clerk of the county court of Cook county shall designate the place of holding such election, and give notice thereof in one or more of the daily papers published in the county of Cook, at least six days preceding such election, and shall supply the judges thereof with the necessary books, papers and boxes, as in other cases of elections; and there shall be one polling or voting place in each voting precinct in said towns, as the same were fixed at the last general election in the county of Cook. The persons who acted as judges or inspectors of election in the several precincts of said towns, at the last general election in Cook county, shall be the judges or inspectors of this election. In case the judges or inspectors of election shall not attend at the time for opening the polls, such judges or inspectors shall be chosen by the legal voters present. The clerk shall be appointed as provided in elections for county officers. The polls shall be opened and closed and the election conducted as the elections for county officers. All legal voters of said towns shall be entitled to vote at such election, without any new registration; and the judges or inspectors of such election shall use the registry list made for the general election in November, 1868: *Provided.* that whenever any person whose name is not on the registry list shall offer his vote at such election, the judges or inspectors shall require the same evidence of his qualification as now provided by law. The said judges of election shall, immediately after the closing of the polls, count the ballots, fill out and sign the returns and tally sheets, as now provided by law in all other elections, and return the poll books and ballots to the clerk of the county court, as in other' cases of election. The votes shall be canvassed in the manner provided by law for the election of state and county officers. The clerk of the county court of Cook county shall, immediately after such canvass, cause a certificate of the result of such election to be filed in the office of Secretary of State, which shall be conclusive evidence of the result of said election.

SEC. 19. This act shall be a public act, and shall take effect and be in force from and after its passage.

— - —

WEST CHICAGO.

AN ACT TO AMEND THE CHARTER OF THE CITY OF CHICAGO, TO CREATE A BOARD OF PARK COMMISSIONERS, AND AUTHORIZE A TAX IN THE TOWN OF WEST CHICAGO, AND FOR OTHER PURPOSES:

SECTION 1. *Be it enacted by the People of the State of Illinois, represented in the General Assembly*, That the territorial limits of the city of Chicago shall be and are hereby extended as follows: That part of Section 36, 40, 14 east of 3d P. M., which lies west of the North Branch of the Chicago River; Section 25, 40, 13 east of 3d P. M., except that part of said section lying east of the center of the North Branch of the Chicago river;

sections 26, 35 and 36, in township 40, 13 east of 3d P. M.: sections 1, 2, 11, 12, 13, 14, 23, 24, 25 and 26, in township 39, 13 east of 3d P. M., and that part of sections 35 and 36, in township 39, 13 east of 3d P. M., lying north-west of the center of the Illinois and Michigan canal, shall be, and are hereby, added to said city, and shall constitute a part of the West Division of said city, and of the town of West Chicago, and the said added or new territory shall cease to be a part of the several towns to which it now belongs or appertains, and the outside boundary of the West Division of the city of Chicago, as hereby established, shall be the outside boundary of the several wards of the city which now extend to the present city limits.

SEC. 2. Seven persons, resident freeholders and qualified voters of said town, who shall be designated by the governor of the state of Illinois, together with their successors, shall be, and they are hereby, constituted a Board of Public Park Commissioners for the town of West Chicago, to be known under the name of the "West Chicago Park Commissioners," and in case of the failure of any of said persons to accept such appointment, and to qualify thereunder as hereinafter provided, within sixty days after the passage of this act, the place of such person in said commission shall be thereby vacated, and it shall be the duty of the commissioners so accepting to certify the fact of such failure and vacancy to the governor, who shall appoint some suitable person or persons, possessing the qualifications aforesaid, to fill the place or places thus made vacant, and vacancies shall continue to be filled in like manner, until the board shall have been filled and constituted by the acceptance and qualification of seven persons. Each of said commissioners, before entering upon the duties of his office, shall take an oath to well and properly discharge the duties of his office for the interest of the public, which oath shall be reduced to writing, subscribed to by him, and filed in the office of the county clerk of Cook county. They shall each give a bond in the penal sum of $20,000, with one or more sureties, to be approved by the judge of the circuit court of Cook county, to the treasurer of Cook county, conditioned for the faithful discharge of their duties under the act.

SEC. 3. As soon as convenient after the said board shall be constituted as aforesaid, the members thereof shall decide by lot, at a meeting to be called by any three of them, as to the respective term for which each member shall hold his office; the number of lots shall equal the number of commissioners, and the person drawing the longest term shall serve seven years from the first day of March, 1869; the one drawing the next shall serve for six years from said date; the one drawing the next shall serve for five years from said date; and so on, until the term of each one of said commissioners shall be definitely determined, each one serving for the length of time inscribed on the lot drawn by him; the last of said commissioners serving for the term of one year only from said first day of March, A. D. 1869. As soon as the term of office of each of said commissioners shall be determined as aforesaid, said board shall organize, by electing one of their number as president, and one of their number as auditor. They shall also appoint a treasurer, prescribe his duties, and fix his compensation, who shall give bond for the faithful discharge of his duties in the penal sum of $50,000, with not less than three sufficient sureties, to be approved by the judge of the circuit court of Cook county. They shall also choose a secretary, who shall not necessarily be a commissioner, and who shall hold his office until his successor shall be appointed, as hereinafter provided; and all officers appointed by the board shall be subject to removal, at the pleasure of the board. The said board shall adopt a seal, and alter the same at pleasure; they shall keep a complete record of all their proceedings, which shall be open at all times for the inspection of the public. The said commissioners shall receive no compensation for their services, except the president, who may, in the discretion of said board, have and receive such compensation as may be fixed, as hereinafter provided, not to exceed four thousand dollars per annum. All vacancies occurring in said board shall be filled as soon as may be thereafter, by the appointment of the governor of the state of Illinois. The said board of commissioners shall be a body politic and corporate, with perpetual succession, and power to sue and be sued, plead and be impleaded, to have and use a common seal, and they shall have and enjoy all the powers necessary for the purposes of this act.

Sec. 4. The said board of commissioners shall have full and exclusive power to govern, manage and direct all parks, boulevards and ways authorized by this act, and by them purchased, made, laid out or established; to lay out, regulate, make and improve the same, to pass ordinances and issue and enforce orders for the regulation and government of the same; to levy special assessments on all property by them deemed benefited by the purchase, opening and improvement of such parks, boulevards and ways, as limited by this act; to appoint such engineers, surveyors, clerks and other officers, including a police force, as may be necessary; to define and prescribe their respective duties and authority, and fix the amount of their compensation; and generally in regard to said parks, boulevards and ways, they shall possess all the power and authority now by law conferred upon or possessed by the common council of the city of Chicago in respect to the public squares, places and streets in said city; and it shall be lawful for them to commence the improvement of the same as soon as the funds requisite therefor, or any portion thereof, shall have been obtained. The expenditure for engineers, surveyors, clerks and officers, except the president, including a police force, shall not exceed five thousand dollars per annum, without further authority from the General Assembly; but said board may accept of the services of such of the police force of the city of Chicago as may be placed at their disposal by the common council or police authorities of said city.

Sec. 5. The said board shall have power, and it shall be made their duty, and they are hereby authorized, to select and take possession of, and to acquire by condemnation, contract, donation or otherwise, title forever, in trust for the inhabitants of the town of West Chicago and of the West Division of Chicago, and for such parties or persons as may succeed to the rights of said inhabitants, and for the public as public promenades and pleasure grounds and ways, but not without the consent of a majority, by frontage, of the owners of the property fronting the same for any other use or purpose, and without the power to sell, alienate. mortgage, or encumber the same. to the lands, and appurtenances required for a road, or pleasure way, or boulevard, not less than two hundred and fifty, nor more than four hundred feet in width, and for the establishment of a building-line, as here-inafter specified. fifty feet distant from and outside of said boulevard or pleasure way, beginning at a point in said added territory north of Fullerton Avenue, and at or near the North Branch of the Chicago River, and extending west within said added territory to a point one mile or more west of Western Avenue, and thence southerly to a point at or near the Illinois and Michigan Canal, with such curves and deviations as they shall deem expedient; also to the lands required and building-lines aforesaid for three parks upon the line of said boulevard, and upon the part of the same between the two last mentioned points, of not less than one hundred nor more than two hundred acres each, and which shall cost respectively not exceeding $250 000; the first to be located north of Kinzie street; the second to be located between Kinzie street and Harrison street. and the third to be located between Harrison street and the Chicago, Burlington & Quincy Railroad track; the total cost of said parks and boulevards. with the easements and building-line aforesaid, exclusive of improvements. shall not exceed $900.000, and shall be assessed on the property benefited as herein-after provided. If the said board should locate any part of said boulevard or parks outside of the said extended territory and limits. each section of land west of the same, of which a part shall be taken for such boulevard or parks, shall be and remain, together with the lands and territory between the same, and the said limits, a part of the said town and city, and of the several wards thereof as aforesaid, and shall cease to be a part of the several towns to which it now belongs or appertains. But in no case shall the western line of either of said parks be over two (2) miles from Western avenue, unless by voluntary contributions land is added to such parks outside of said limits. Said lands, boulevards and parks, and the personal property of said board shall be exempt from taxation. The said board may contract with the owners of property taken or purchased, for annual payments, not to extend beyond five years, and in such case shall only include in the assessment for any year that amount of such annual payments then due, if any, and the amount of one annual payment for that year, or next to become due. They are also authorized to divide the amount of their assessments, and where it can legally be done, to make one or more assessments, payable in annual installments, which shall be a lien on property only for the amount payable each year. The part of said boulevards between the said North Park and the North Branch of the Chicago River, and the part of the same south of the said Chicago, Burling-ton & Quincy Railroad track, shall not be made unless the land therefor shall be acquired free of cost to said board, and shall not be ornamented or improved until after the improvement of the parks shall have been com-pleted. unless the same be done by voluntary contribntion.

SEC. 6. The establishment of a building-line outside of said boulevard

C

and parks as hereinbefore required in connection with the condemnation of
the land for the same shall be understood to be the condemnation and
perpetual annihilation of all right of the owners of property which shall
front on said boulevard, or across which said building-line shall run, to
erect any building whatever or any part thereof, between said building-line
and said boulevard or parks; or it may be accomplished by the absolute
condemnation of the land, with perpetual and irrevocable free license to use
and occupy fifty feet in width of the same for all purposes not otherwise
forbidden, except building, as the said board shall be advised may be
preferable and most effective.

SEC. 7. No subdivision into lots of any lands in said town lying within
four hundred feet of said boulevard, or either of said parks, shall be valid
without the approval of the said Board of Park Commissioners, and they
also shall have power to forbid by general order, and to abate any horse-
racing, gambling, or offensive or obnoxious or dangerous business or amuse-
ments, within four hundred feet of said boulevard and parks, or either of
them, and the right to use the said adjacent lands for any such purposes
shall be deemed to be included in the assessment and condemnation above
provided for. But no lawful business now established and carried on upon
said adjacent lands shall be prohibited or abated without a fair valuation and
due and full compensation.

SEC. 8. The said board shall have power to construct all necessary
bridges and viaducts, over rivers, water courses and railroads within or on
the line of said town, and it shall be their duty to construct the same as soon
as the means shall have been provided therefor.

SEC. 9. The said Board of Park Commissioners are hereby required to
make not less than three topographical surveys and examinations of different
routes for said boulevards and outlines of parks, with complete elevations,
before locating the same, and to invite owners of property to confer with
them in regard to donations of land. They are also authorized to receive
donations or appropriations of money for the purchase or improvement of
the same, and of lands for, or as a part of or to be added to said boulevard
or either of said park, upon conditions to be agreed upon.

SEC. 10. None of the main streets and avenues leading to the said
boulevard and parks, and which have heretofore been opened and used as
country roads or highways, shall ever be closed up or reduced in width, in
whole or in part, except streets near the river and its branches, which may be
changed for business purposes or greater convenience of access. The Board
of Public Works are hereby authorized and required, upon the order of the
Common Council, to make and assess, in the manner herein and in the city
charter provided, subject to confirmation by the Common Council, the
benefits and damages resulting from the extension of the road known as
"Whiskey Point Road," as nearly as may be in its present direction, from
its present western terminus at Western avenue, to Fulton street, of the
width of 120 feet, and from Fulton street to Lake street of the width of 80
feet, and the widening said road from its present terminus at Western avenue
to the new or extended city limits, to the width of 120 feet, with a building

line as hereinbefore defined and specified, distant ten feet from, and outside of each line of said road from Fulton street to Western avenue, and 50 feet from and outside of said road from Western avenue to the new or extended city limits, and also the grading and macadamizing said road or the middle part thereof, to the width of at least 30 feet, and a viaduct or viaducts for carriages, teams and foot passengers, over all railroad tracks now laid or hereafter to be laid across said road. The several township road officers and the Cook County Drainage Commissioners, and all other officers now or hereafter authorized to open roads on said line outside of the city limits, in making any assessment for widening said road, are authorized and required to include the establishment of said building line fifty feet distant from and outside of said road, as aforesaid The name of the said " Whiskey Point Road, " both within and beyond said city limits, shall be and is hereby changed, and shall be known forever hereafter as " Grand Avenue." The Southwestern avenue, from Madison street to the city limits, shall also be macadamized, with the consent and approval of the Common Council.

SEC. 11. In case the said commissioners cannot agree with the owner or owners, lessees or occupants of any of the said real estate, selected by them as aforesaid, they may proceed to procure the condemnation of the same in the manner prescribed in the act of the General Assembly of the State of Illinois, entitled, " An act to amend the law condemning right of way for the purpose of internal improvements, approved January 22, 1852," and the acts then in force amendatory thereof; the provisions of which said act, and the several acts amendatory thereof, are hereby extended to the boulevards, parks and Park Commissioners, to be created by virtue of this act.

SEC. 12. When the title of the land selected for boulevards, ways, ease-ments, parks and building lines as herein provided, shall have been acquired by the Commissioners, by gift, condemnation, or otherwise, it shall be the duty of such Commissioners to make, acknowledge and file for record, in the office of the Recorder of Deeds for Cook county, a map showing the said land, with a correct description, including section, township and range.

SEC. 13. As soon as the amount required for the condemnation of the grounds selected for said purposes shall have been ascertained by said commissioners, with reasonable certainty, they shall apply to the judge of the circuit court of Cook county, for the appointment of three disinter-ested freeholders, as assessors, one of whom shall reside north of Division street, one between Division and Harrison streets, and one south of Harrison street, all in said West Chicago. The commissioners shall give notice in three or more of the daily newspapers published in the city of Chicago, and by posting written or printed notices in three public places in said West Chicago, of the time when such application will be made, and all parties interested may appear and be heard by the said judge, touching such appointment, at the time fixed for such application. The court, after hearing such persons as shall desire to be heard touching such appointment, shall nominate and appoint three assessors, qualified as aforesaid, for the purpose provided in this act. The said assessors shall proceed to assess the

amount so ascertained upon the property by them deemed benefited by
reason of the improvement occasioned by the location of said boulevard
and parks, with their appurtenances, as near as may be in proportion to the
benefits resulting thereto, and also the damages, if any, occasioned by the
taking, or condemnation of any land, right or easement as aforesaid; and
in general the form and particulars of the assessment shall be as near as may
be the same required by the city charter of Chicago in the condemnation of
land for, and the laying out of streets. From the funds derived from said
assessment, and from the other funds of said board applicable to such
purposes, the said board shall pay to the parties entitled thereto the amounts
respectively due them, and thereupon the title of the said lands, ways,
boundary lines, easements and parks, or that portion thereof paid for as
aforesaid, shall become fixed and vested in said board and their successors
in the manner, to the extent, for the purposes, and subject to the limitations,
hereinbefore provided. Upon entering upon the duties of their office, the
said assessors shall make oath before the clerk of the circuit court faithfully
and impartially to discharge the duties of their office; they shall give at least
ten days' notice, in three of the said daily papers, and by posting notices as
aforesaid, of the time and place of their meeting for the purpose of making
said assessment, and may adjourn said meeting from time to time, until the
same shall be completed. In making said assessment, the said assessors
shall estimate the value of the several lots, blocks or parcels of land deemed
benefited by them as aforesaid, and shall include the same, together with the
amount assessed as benefits, in the assessment roll. All parties interested
may appear before said assessors, and be heard touching any matter connected with the assessment. When the same shall be completed, it shall be
signed by the assessor, and returned to the said circuit court, and shall be
filed by the clerk thereof. The assessors shall thereupon give at least ten
days' notice, in three of the said daily newspapers, and by posting notices
as aforesaid, of the filing of said assessment roll, and that they will, on a
day therein named, apply to the circuit court for confirmation of the same,
which said notice shall be published at least ten days before the time fixed
for such application. Said circuit court shall have power to revise, correct,
amend or confirm said assessment, in whole or in part, and may make or
order a new assessment, in whole or in part, and the same revise and confirm
upon like notice. All parties may appear before said circuit court, either in
person or by attorney, when such application shall be made, and may object
to said assessment, either in whole or in part, provided all objections shall
be in writing, and shall be filed at least three days before the time fixed for
the application, and shall specify the lot, block or parcels of land on behalf
of which objection is made. After the confirmation of said assessment, the
clerk of said court shall file a copy thereof, under the seal of said court, with
the clerk of the county court of Cook county, and said assessment shall be
a lien upon the several lots, blocks or parcels of land assessed for benefits as
aforesaid. The clerk of the said Cook county court shall include in the
general warrants for each year, until the assessments for the purposes
authorized by this act shall have been completed, and until the whole

sum shall be paid, for the collection of state and county taxes in the said town of West Chicago, the said assessment, in an appropriate column, to be termed "West Park and Boulevard Assessment," with the amount to be collected opposite the several lots, blocks or parcels of land assessed as aforesaid, and like proceedings, in all respects, shall be had for enforcing the same as are now provided by law for the collection of state and county taxes. The moneys collected under the provisions of this section shall be paid to the treasurer of Cook county, for which he and his sureties shall be responsible, as fully as for any other moneys by him received as treasurer of Cook county, and be held by him in the same manner, and be subject to the same control and direction, as provided in this act for other moneys belonging to said corporation. And the treasurer of Cook county shall be entitled to receive one-half of one per cent., and no more, of said moneys, as a full compensation for receiving and disbursing the same.

SEC. 14. If deemed practicable by the assessors, separate assessments and appraisements shall be made, one for that part of the said boulevard, ways, building line and easements, and for said park, building line and easements, to be made and taken North of Division street; one for the same between Division street and Harrison street, and one for the same south of Harrison street. The benefits assessed shall be the real and appreciable benefits, and the assessments shall not, in any case, be extended over any land, lots or parts of the said West Chicago where said benefits do not exist. No assessment for boulevard or park improvement shall be made until further authorized by the General Assembly.

SEC. 15. For the expense authorized herein for surveys and for any deficiencies and necessary outlays arising and required in the condemnation aforesaid, and in the purchase of lands and property for the purposes herein specified, and for the payment of the expenses of maintaining and improving the said boulevard and parks, and of enclosing the same when deemed necessary, and for draining and making roadways and walks upon the same, and for other expenses, disbursements, and changes in the premises, said commissioners shall have power to borrow, as they shall deem expedient, an amount of money not exceeding $50,000 in the aggregate, and for a time not exceeding three years, and at a rate of interest not exceeding ten per cent. per annum, and to issue therefor the notes or obligations of the said corporation, which shall be numbered consecutively from number one, and shall be signed by the president and countersigned by the secretary of said board, and shall be registered accurately and minutely in a register which shall at all times be open for the examination of the public, and no note or obligation made as aforesaid shall be valid for an amount exceeding the sum remaining of said $50,000 as appears by said register, or until the same shall have been duly registered in said register. For the payment of the principal and interest of said notes and obligations, the town of West Chicago shall be irrevocably pledged, and also the proceeds of the tax hereinafter authorized.

SEC. 16. The adoption of the proposition for boulevard and parks as hereinafter specified, shall be deemed and taken to be the consent of the said town of West Chicago to the imposition of an annual tax of one-half of one mill for boulevard and park purposes, as hereinafter provided. It shall be the duty of the clerk of the county court of Cook county to set down in the general tax warrants of each year, for the collection of state and county taxes, in a separate column, a tax of one-half of one mill, to be styled "Boulevard and Park Tax," which is hereby levied upon all the taxable property in said town of West Chicago, and shall set down in said column the amount of said tax chargeable to the several persons, corporations, lots, or parcels of land liable for taxes in said town; and the collector shall proceed to collect the same in the manner now provided by law for the collection of state and county taxes; and all the provisions of law in respect to the collection of state and county taxes, and proceedings to enforce the same, so far as applicable, shall apply to said assessments and taxes. The said sums of money shall be placed by the treasurer of said county of Cook to the credit of said board, and shall be drawn by said board from the county treasury by a warrant, signed by the president and secretary of said board, and countersigned by the auditor to be appointed as aforesaid, and in no other way. The appointment of such auditor shall be first certified by such president and secretary, and filed in the office of said treasurer of Cook county.

SEC. 17. It shall be lawful for said commissioners to vacate and close up any and all public roads or highways, excepting railroads, for commercial purposes, which may pass through, divide or separate any lands selected or appropriated by them for the purposes of a park, and no such road shall ever be laid out through said park, except such as the said commissioners shall lay out and construct: *Provided, however,* that neither Lake street, Madison nor Twelfth streets, nor either of the diagonal avenues or roads leading into said city, nor any boulevard nor horse railway track of any person or corporation now authorized to make the same, shall be closed under the provisions of this section, but the same may be worked and controlled when, and so far as, within the lines of either of said parks, by the said board, but without interrupting travel over the same.

SEC. 18. The said commissioners, or either of them, may be removed from office by the circuit court of said county, after trial and conviction, upon the petition, with sworn charges, presented by not less than ten reputable freeholders of said town of West Chicago, and if it shall appear at said trial that the said commissioner or commissioners have been guilty of misdemeanor or malfeasance in office under this act; and if the said court shall remove any of said commissioners from office for any such cause, before the expiration of his or their term of office, the clerk of said court shall certify to the governor of the state of Illinois, under the seal of the court, a copy of the final judgment of removal. The president and secretary of the board shall certify to the governor all other vacancies arising or occurring in the same after the organization thereof.

SEC. 19. The office of any commissioner under this act, who shall not attend meetings of the board for three successive months, after having been duly notified of said meetings, without reasons satisfactory to the board, or without leave of absence from said board, may, by said board, be declared, and thereupon shall become, vacant.

SEC. 20. There shall be an election held in the town of West Chicago on the fourth Tuesday of March next, after the passage of this act at which election the legal voters voting at said election shall vote for or against the creation of the said Board of Park Commissioners, the laying out and making of said boulevards and parks, with their appurtenances, the addition of said sections of land above described by numbers, to said city and town of West Chicago and the extension of the limits thereof, and the imposition of the tax hereby declared to be levied, at which all legal voters residing in the said added territory shall have the right to vote. The tickets shall be printed or written "For the Boulevards and Parks," and "Against the Boulevards and Parks," and if the majority of the votes cast on the question shall be "For the Boulevards and Parks," then the propositions in the first part of this section specified shall be held to be consented to and voted by the said town, and all the provisions of this act relating thereto shall take effect and be in force, with the other provisions of this act, but not other-wise: *Provided, however,* That there shall be open in the said territory added from the town of Jefferson, at the house of Henry Jewell, known as "Powell's Tavern," a poll for the casting of the votes of said last mentioned territory separately, at which election M. N. Kimbell, John F. Powell and John Hise shall be judges of election, and the legal voters resident therein on the tenth (10) day of February, A. D. 1869, may vote for "City Exten-sion." and "Against City Extension," and "For the Boulevards and Parks," and "Against the Boulevards and Parks," and if a majority of the votes so cast shall be "Against City Extension," and "Against the Boulevards and Parks," then the territory herein taken from said town of Jefferson, shall not become a part of the city of Chicago, or of the town of West Chicago, nor shall the jurisdiction of said city be extended over the same, but the same shall remain a part of the town of Jefferson, the same as if this act had not been passed, and said vote shall not be counted with or affect the vote cast in the remaining territory embraced in this act. The clerk of the county court of Cook county shall, exept as herein otherwise provided, designate the places of holding such election, and give notice thereof in three or more of the daily newspapers published in the county of Cook, at least ten days preceding such election, and shall supply the judges thereof with the necessary books, papers and boxes, as in other cases of elections; and there shall be one polling or voting place in each voting district in said town, as the same were fixed at the last general election in the county of Cook. The persons who acted as judges or inspectors of election in the several districts of said town, at the last general election in Cook county, shall be the judges or inspectors of this election. In case the judges or inspectors of election shall not attend at the time for opening the polls, such judges or inspectors shall be chosen by the legal voters present. In case it shall be necessary to do so, the said clerk of the county court shall prescribe districts and appoint places of voting in the added territory aforesaid, at which the legal voters present shall choose the judges or inspectors of election. The clerks shall be appointed as provided in elections for county officers. The polls shall be opened and closed and the election conducted, as elections for county officers. All legal voters of said town shall be entitled to vote at such election, without any registration; and the judges or inspectors of such election shall use the registered list made for the general election in November, A. D. 1868: and where necessary to do so, said county clerk shall obtain copies of such registry lists of the several towns from which the said added territory is taken, and furnish them in due time at the place or places where the vote of the voters of the said added territory shall be taken: *Provided*, That whenever any person whose name is not on the registry list shall offer his vote at such election, the judges or inspectors shall require the same evidence of his qualification as now provided by law. The said judges of election shall immediately after the close of the polls, count the ballots, fill out and sign the returns and tally sheets as now provided by law in all other elections, and return the poll books and ballots to the clerk of the county court, as in other cases of election. The votes shall be canvassed in the manner provided by law for the election of state and county officers. The clerk of the county court of Cook county shall, immediately after such canvass, cause a certificate of the result of such election to be filed in the office of the Secretary of State, which shall be conclusive evidence of the result of said election.

Sec. 21. This act shall be deemed a public act, and shall be in force from and after its passage. It shall be liberally construed in all courts and places, and all acts and parts of acts in conflict with its provisions or either of them, are hereby repealed.

www.ingramcontent.com/pod-product-compliance
Lightning Source LLC
Chambersburg PA
CBHW032149010726
47493CB00008BA/2639